Best of 2025
Volume One

WELL READ Magazine

Edited by Mandy Haynes

WELL READ Magazine's BEST OF 2025 Volume One

Published by three dogs write press

Cover art by Malcolm Glass

Cover & Interior Design by Mandy Haynes

979-8-9898952-6-7 (paperback)

979-8-9898952-8-1 (e-book)

For everyone with a story to share and to the readers waiting to read them.

TABLE OF CONTENTS

0

Introduction

In January of 2023, *WELL READ Magazine* began accepting submissions for prose, poetry, and visual art. I was blown away by all of the talented poets, authors, and artists that first year and that feeling of excitement I get when reading a new submission hasn't changed a bit in the last three years. If anything, it's gotten stronger. I can't explain how good it feels to share them with readers every month through the online journal, and how much I look forward to publishing the annual anthologies.

Because the submissions are too good not to share again—in print—to give readers another chance to find them. There are no prompts or themes for the submissions so I never know what I'm getting into until I dive in. Every submission is a surprise and each one hits you in a different way. I love that rollercoaster ride feeling with each new entry, so I've broken the traditional rules for publishing collections and kept the anthologies in the same format as what you find in the online journal. You never know what's coming next so get ready for a fun ride!

In the *Best of 2025 Volume One*, you'll find forty-one submissions written by a fantastic mix of award-winning authors and poets plus new ones to the scene. Five submissions in this volume were nominated for a Pushcart Prize: *Why I Said What I Said to the Bartender* by Alaina Hammond, *The Easter Dress* by Dawn Major, *Montecito* by Leslie Zemeckis, *Dream Merchant* by Francine Rodriguez, and *Stagnation* by Rachid Toumi. The cover art is a photograph by artist, Malcolm Glass, who had several pieces published in October of 2024. You can find that issue and all past issues here www.issuu.com/wellreadmagazine.

If you have a story, essay, poem, or artwork you would like to submit for consideration in upcoming issues of *WELL READ Magazine*, I would love to hear from you. Visit the website and find the submission guidelines under the Call for Submissions tab in the menu.

As always - thanks for reading!

Mandy Haynes
Editor-in-Chief of *WELL READ Magazine*

Did You Ever Get Back Home?

J. B. Hogan

Did you ever get back home,
was it as great as you remembered?
Did it take out the longing,
the agitation that you felt?
Was it all that you wanted,
or are you longing still?
Was geography the problem,
or something broken inside?
How long did you have to wait
to find your way back home?
How does it feel there now,
are you happy at last?
Was this really the answer
to what stirred inside –
or just another misdirection
on an uncertain road that never ends?

Dummy in a Guard Shack

Steve Putnam

"I'm calling to report your guard looks like he's lifeless."

As if the guard needs a ventriloquist, I hear a woman's voice come back over the intercom. "He's a real dummy." The voice sounds detached, unconcerned about my concern for a lifeless guard who might be alive, for a real-life guard who might be dead.

Calling a fellow employee, a real dummy in front of a visitor sounds like a violation of some unwritten code. I'm almost ready to call 911 myself. The guard's sitting back, legs crossed, relaxed as if he's about to laugh at a joke that no one told. He doesn't look dead. He doesn't look like a dummy or mannequin.

"Your mission?" the voice asks

"I'm your technician. Dispatch dispatched me. You are?" I ask.

"Stella," she replies.

This is today's last call. I'm running late, lost time checking out a dead machine that had lost power. I traced the problem using a meter, only to discover the obvious, a power strip switch in the off position.

I'm the new guy, three weeks on the job, the first time riding solo. Dispatch sends the new guy to the calls nobody else wants, low priority, billable printers, end of contract equipment owned by disloyal customers who signed on with the competition. Marginal clients who pay billables six months late. Complainers who expect the best from yesterday's technology. The only way out of this rut is to figure out which dispatcher I need to bribe with bagels.

It's dusk. In the dim light, the guard appears to be asleep. Baseball cap brim pulled over his forehead, I can't tell for sure. Maybe he's dead for good. Maybe he's catnapping, ready to genuflect if someone catches him sleeping on watch. How could he be fired for praying? My most generous assessment, he's a victim of sleep deprivation, or worse, narcolepsy.

The guard shack plate-glass window closed; I try yelling. "Is anyone home?"

The woman's soft voice again, cautious, "Home is where the heart is. Your mission, please?"

A graduate of a one-day charm school on how to treat customers, I keep my analytic thoughts to myself. Home is where the heart is—only if the heart still beats. "What kind of mission? I need to know more to answer your question. Would you consider telling me why you called?" I too am cautious. I would like to help save the man who might be lifeless. I'd like to get on with my last assignment.

"We don't want any funny business—scrappers, you know, copper wire and pipe stealers."

I understand why a power company would want to hang on to its copper wiring. But something is strange. Only two cars, an old Chevy HHR that's a cheap imitation of a fifties delivery van, and road-worn Toyota without registration plates occupy the parking lot, a couple of hundred spaces. The Switchfield Power Plant sign remains on the side of the brick building; the company must have gone under.

"Our main entrance is closed for security," the woman says. "Park by the side door. I'll meet you there."

If Switchfield Power's defunct, why worry about scrappers? If it's still a business, where are the cars that belong to people who run the coal conveyors from train cars to coal grinders to the furnaces? The valve turners that control the water to the boilers, the control room gauge watchers, electricians, plumbers, mechanics. What about a few desk jockeys?

Driving toward the parking lot, I approach a hose stretched across the driveway. An alarm bell rings when the wheels cross, it's the same kind that alerted gas station attendants whenever a customer arrived.

The side door's locked, I wait. The same, almost mesmerizing soft voice on an overhead speaker. "Who goes there?"

I can't tell if she needs to know or if she's joking. Guard shack guy she calls dummy already has me confused. "Machine Repair." I hope my voice sounds professional. "It's what I do."

The woman opening the door has the same intercom voice. "Oh! You're the funny guy who wanted to save our dummy," she says her smirk almost a smile. She seems more friendly than I expected.

"I can't call anyone, 'dummy.' Employee handbook forbids it."

"We do and say everything we can to keep our visitors from calling 911," the woman says.

Her words are precise as if she's making a public service announcement that discourages false alarms. She too is wearing a security uniform like the guard at the guard shack without a gate. Dark blue pants and a polo shirt, same dark blue as the guard's uniform, a Switchfield Security patch on her left sleeve. Her blond hair tied back, she looks like a cute woman trying to look unattractive.

I try not to dwell on the fact that security always makes me insecure. After all, this is not about me. But there is something about this place that's out of the ordinary, strange. It tweaks my attention the way that Ritalin worked when I was in school.

The guard leads the way. The place reminds me of a faded picture in some outdated seventh-grade science book. Only stairs and catwalks leading to the office are lit by electric light bulbs enclosed in dingy glass globes. Wire cables bundled in the gloomy chill, open steel stairs from level to level, steel crosswalks from side to side. Asbestos-clad pipes rise upward, branch outward, creating continuous interconnections, a maze for steam to find its way to giant turbines to power enclosed generators.

Everything you need to make electricity, there's nothing—no sound of fire, turning shafts, high voltage hum. "Why the security to protect such a wasteland," I ask.

"It's just a wasteland in need of transformation. We're the custodians."

"We?"

"We, we." Again, that smirk.

"We we?" I ask back. I can't tell if she's talking in French or making fun of my English.

"My father and I run Security."

"What about the guard? Did you call 911?"

"The guard's our first line of defense."

"The pneumatic hose that rings the bell, the second line?"

"You could say that. This way," she says, motioning me to follow.

I follow her up another steel stairway, across another rusty catwalk. Rust-stained turbines below, I look upward to find where the roof leaks.

"Custodians?" I ask. "Exactly what is it that you care for? Why are you here?"

"That's an existential question. We are here because the plant is here."

"Why is the plant still here?"

"It went tapioca; the bank shut it down, repoed the real estate. They're waiting for science to come up with a way to make asbestos miraculously disappear."

"I don't know the going rate for bankrupt electric plants. It looks useless to me."

"You're right. It is worthless. But our job is to maintain the status quo—the worthlessness if you will. The only thing that makes worthlessness worse—deterioration makes it a greater financial liability?"

"What about foreign investors?" I ask.

"They're too smart to waste their time. They go after hotels with tarnished names."

"Where do Americans invest?"

"Foreign investments."

"Who pays for the custodians?"

"The bank does. Our presence stabilizes the projected loss on this place as a worthless asset."

"How can a loser be called an asset?"

"Calling it an asset provides cover to potential investors."

"So, you said you're custodians—you and your father. What a coincidence. How did you both get a job without qualifications?"

Stella laughs. "Are you writing a book? You ask a lot of questions—OK. My father worked here forever. He was on the crew that shut things down. Put it into mothballs. They shut off the water supply and steam supply valves. Shipped out coal cars still loaded with coal. Who knows where the coal ended up? My father's the one who locked the doors."

"So how did you get a job here?"

"My father knew the right people. We are not workers. We are contractors who specialize in deterioration control. This was a cutting-edge opportunity. Right place right time."

"And you bought a dummy?" I hope I don't sound wiseass. It's an opening for Stella to admit the dummy in the guardhouse is some intellectual lightweight who managed to hold on to his job. Or she could admit it's a real dummy. Corporate survivors lead complicated lives, either way.

"If you need to know, the guard's name is Oscar. He remains in the guard shack."

We reach a door, lettered in some kind of techno-slanted font: ‘Security and Reindustrialization.’

“How can a bank industrialize a place appraised as worthless?”

Stella sighs as if she’s even getting more tired of my questions. She opens the door. The Department of Security and Industrialization appears to be located in an old facility shop, half of the space loaded with antique lathes, drills, hydraulic presses, grinders, micrometers, and calipers. Rows of shelves filling the other half display crude toy-like contraptions, thin copper wire coils suspended on small wooden platforms, complete with alligator clips, ready to hook to a power source.

An old man who must be Stella’s father perches on a stool at a metal workbench. He winds a coil around a short length of pipe, removes it, and ties it off so it holds its circular shape. Thinner than any of the copper wire I’ve seen here at Switchfield electric, the wire must come from an outside source.

Stella doesn’t introduce me to the old man, so I reach out, extending my hand. “Don’t bother,” she says. He stopped talking after the change.”

“What change?

“Burning coal to boil water to make steam to turn the turbines to drive the generators, pushing out power to the people. You never saw much of the fire or steam and you never saw the electricity. But you knew if you touched a cable, you’d fry. That’s what the old reality was.

“Then the change. the plant shutdown. His friends of forty and fifty years left. His job description changed from machinist to head of security. He couldn’t handle the nothingness of a life that didn’t require him to be industrious, the guilt of surviving the layoff. The whole thing almost drove him crazy”

My eyes turn toward the coils suspended over the wooden pedestals. “The motors?” I ask, pointing. What do you do with them all?”

No surprise, the old man ignores me.

"Toy motors," Stella says. "It's too bad my father doesn't have grandchildren. He builds them, tests them, runs them on the shelf. It doesn't matter that they're a hard sell. It's part of the contract. One solar panel on the roof powers the motors. It might qualify as a tax write-off to stabilize the liability. It's proof to the bank and tax people that our business is legit. Believe it or not, magnetism is supposedly therapeutic."

Sure enough, the old man hooks the alligator clips to a power supply, gently nudges the coil with his index finger. Magic, miracle, or laws of gravity, electricity, and magnetism, the coil spins. He sits back as if contented with tracing the circle of life in the rotating coils.

His bench displays a collection of vintage voltage, ohm, ammeters, and multimeters. Shelves and shelves of more and more motors with geometric coils, circular and spiraled, shafted vertically or horizontally. The crude motors defy predictability, fast and slow, some wobble. "Sometimes the magic works, sometimes it doesn't," Stella says. "Since he doesn't talk, he has time to keep notes."

Instead of industrial satisfaction or amusement, the motors might be the therapeutic result of paradoxical intention. In concert working together, maybe the whirling magnetic coils provide enough TMS, Transcranial Magnetic Stimulation to treat depression. It could be my imagination. At the moment at least, I'm feeling better than I felt when I arrived. Stella looks cute to me when she's not smirking.

The printer has a weird but interesting problem. The machine's display shows a jam at the paper exit. Even while I'm troubleshooting, the jam indicator goes light then dark as if there's jammed paper mysteriously coming and going. After considerable effort, I find a spider slow dancing with life on a photosensor, located right before the exit tray. It's something you can't make up, but who would believe me? Dead or alive, Oscar's out in the guard shack. There's no way he'd understand if I told him. The old man who can't or won't talk wouldn't want to hear anything from me. Naturally, Stella is the only one I can trust. I surprise myself, telling her a story of a cold factory spider that finds a warm home. Although its new life is in a cushy printer in a facility shop, the spider feels threatened enough to silently cry out for help.

"What did you do with it," Stella asks, her voice more compassionate than usual.

I open an old aspirin bottle that I found on a shelf full of odds and ends. I show her the spider, promising to turn it loose in a place more environmentally friendly than Switchfield Electric.

"Do I need to sign out with Oscar?" I ask.

"There's no need to sign out," Stella assures me. "Professional courtesy only requires that you make Oscar aware of your departure."

"It would hurt his feelings if I didn't?" I still want some assurance that the dummy is real—or unreal, well or not well.

Stella laughs. "A live-security guard would make people wonder, why the security? A dummy would be too unremarkable, at best a bad joke—a cruel prank, possibly from a bitter worker on the shutdown crew?"

Out on the catwalk, shutting the door, I wonder if I'm imagining things when I hear a voice that sounds like it might belong to the old man.

At the guard shack, the guard still looks like a dummy. He's sitting upright now, his head turned slightly toward me. Real or unreal, illumination by a dim nightlight would make him a difficult assassination target. Stella's voice comes through the intercom, "How's Oscar?'

Is she messing with me, I wonder? "Oscar seems fine. How are you, Stella?"

Silence. Could this be a beginning of a love story that takes place on the outskirts of human development, a place where motors motor in a battle between science and reality, accomplishing nothing? Defunct, Switchfield Power Company; the old man, daughter, and I triangulated strangers? Is the old man committed to job satisfaction he only imagines? A daughter's life lost taking care of her father. Me heading home to the comfort of an empty garret apartment.

Originally published in Main Street Rag Spring 2023 Issue

Changes

Gregg Norman

Scars on skin
see changes

Epiphanies
sea changes

From cradle to grave
rolling over me
like rogue tides

One day following
a herd of longhorns
the next day reading Yeats

Life's cabinet
of curiosities

Anything to avoid sameness
the mundane buzz of homogeneity

Living upstairs
in the brain's attic

Guarding my spirit
against humdrummery

The monotone musings
of the masses

Tedium in the medium

Driving myself outward
onward and upward

to new pursuits
passions devised

by a restless soul
and an unsettled psyche

I'll die wanting
to be someone else

Cornbread Communion

Deborah-Zenha Adams

I was a sprout when Granddaddy taught me the best way to eat beans. Here's how it's done: Spoon some pintos and a little of their soup onto the plate, preferably one with big pink flowers and green leaves in the pattern. Smash the beans with the back of a fork. Crumble some cornbread on top, saving the crust to enjoy by itself. Then cover the beans and bread with ketchup (store-bought), and mash it all together.

On my grandparents' farm, this meal might be dinner, which began precisely at 11 a.m., or it might be supper, eaten at the end of the day after the chores were done. Maybe both. There would be other things on the table—corn or potatoes, perhaps, and pork in one form or another. This was a farm where vegetables and hogs were raised for food, where a little cotton was raised for cash, and where grandchildren were raised only during brief summer visits.

My parents left their respective farms and back-breaking farming lifestyle when they married. By the time they produced the first grandchild (me), they'd settled into a residential neighborhood within walking distance of the courthouse square. There was a telephone (exchange YUkon 6) and the highest of technology, a television, from which I learned the music of Dinah Shore ("See the U.S.A….") and the shadow of Alfred Hitchcock.

Back on the farm, Grandmammy went on cooking beans and cornbread on her wood-burning cookstove and drawing icy-cold water from the well, which was enclosed just off the screened back porch, so even when rain poured down, we could drink our fill and clean our hands with lye soap and wash our hair with Grandmammy's Prell shampoo while keeping the rest of us dry.

There was still a circuit preacher at the church, the one my grandparents attended because it was closest to their home and not because they cared or didn't about the doctrine. Sometimes my visits coincided with Sacrament Sunday. My grandmother was responsible for the saltine crackers and grape juice served in communion, such tiny bits, not even enough to slake the hunger or thirst of a little girl. Ah, but afterward the plate and cups came back home with us, and while Grandmammy washed up, I polished off the leftovers, nibbling crackers and taking tiny thimble-cups of juice because a sip tastes better than a gulp.

In every memory I have of farm Sundays, my grandmother served fried chicken. Always. Maybe it was a tender hen, in honor of the visiting preacher, or—if it was only family eating that day—an old hen past her prime laying years.

Washing up and cleaning, cooking and sewing, gardening and preserving…these were my grandmother's domain. She fed the chickens and gathered their eggs, never letting me reach into the nests because there might be a snake or possibly because my small fingers might drop breakfast.

Once a week, Grandmammy would build a fire under the massive black iron pot in the back yard and heat water for washing clothes. Once a year, that same pot would boil the innards of a hog that hung nearby, drained of lifeblood and preserved as ham, sausage, feet and jowls, chitlins, cracklins, and brains.

Granddaddy's first job of the day was milking the cow, who had no official name because she was not a pet. There may have been—must have been—different cows over the years, but they are all one in my memory. And even though there was daily milk, I never met a calf nor saw one in the field or barn. There was only Cow, who eyed me with contempt that one time Granddaddy tried to teach me to milk. Not a drop was produced by the ineffectual squeezing and pulling of my toddler hands. No matter; I never cared for milk or butter, anyway.

Now I'm older by far than my grandparents were then. Corrupted by worldly living, I turned vegetarian, so there's no chicken or pig on my plate. Once or twice a month I treat myself to beans with ketchup and cornbread. My hands don't hover over the plate or invoke the spirit of a mischievous grandfather to bless the meal, nor do I eat in reverent silence. Memory is the only prayer I need.

Originally appeared in The Dead Mule School of Southern Literature, April 2021

My Family of Origin

Rita Welty Bourke

My sister Mae, the girl on the left in the photograph, contracted smallpox when she was six. She recovered but was left with scars on her face. They're called pockmarks. It's one of the few pictures I have of Mae. I keep it on my living room wall above the piano.

The little boy beside her is my brother Bob. He's wearing short pants and squinting at the sun. His hair is long and curly; my mother hated to cut it. He had mumps when he was a child. His glands were so swollen he could hardly eat.

Next in line is my father, who came down with undulant fever from drinking raw milk. I remember the spiking fevers, how he would come in from the field wringing wet, headache so bad all he could do was sit in a rocking chair with his head in his hands. My mother would bring him a wet cloth.

On days when he was not so sick, he would joke that of course he'd recover, that he had at least as much money as Henry Ford. Ford's only son, Edsel, had been diagnosed with the same condition.

Dad was wrong on both counts. We had very little money, and Edsel died of undulant fever. He'd contracted the disease after drinking unpasteurized milk from his father's dairy.

When the family physician came to our farm bringing an envelope containing an experimental drug called Tetracycline, Dad was willing to try it. I think he'd have tried just about anything to be relieved of the sweating, the headaches, the muscle and joint pain. He signed the consent form releasing the manufacturer from liability and thanked the doctor for bringing the medicine. Now there was hope.

I think the doctor's name was Kadel. Maybe it was Cadel. I never saw his name written down.

The drug worked. Within a week the intermittent fevers were gone, as were the headaches. The grated onions my mother had tied to the bottoms of his feet and under his arms—to draw out the poison, our dentist friend had promised—were tossed to the chickens.

But our cattle were infected with brucellosis, the disease that causes undulant fever in humans. Where had it come from? We didn't know. Only that the herd had tested free of both brucellosis and tuberculosis for years. Our suspicions fell on a neighbor who had sold my father two dairy cows. It had been a foolish thing to do, my father said, to buy those untested cattle. He should have asked to see the U.S.D.A. Notice of Certification. He hadn't. Now he was faced with the prospect of losing the herd it had taken years to build.

He took to walking out into the fields, hands clasped behind his back. He was as troubled as I'd ever seen him.

My mother bought a two-gallon steel container that pasteurized the milk we drank. It raised the temperature of the milk to just below boiling, held it there for five minutes, then let it cool.

When we drank it, it tasted burnt.

They came and took the cattle away, all but one. Sugar Baby had tested negative. We were thrilled. Sugar Baby was a pet and we loved her. Months later, she was tested again, and this time she was positive. She was loaded onto a truck; we watched until the truck pulled out onto Route 15, turned southward, and geared up. When it was lost in the haze of the Blue Ridge Mountain Range, we turned away.

Our barn was empty. The barn cats missed the milk my father always poured for them, but they were able to catch mice, and most of them survived. Some crossed the road in search of food. It was a busy highway; when morning came, we often found their bodies.

The little girl on the far right is Rose. Her hair is in finger-curls. When she was 15, she contracted polio. She was crying when Dad picked her up from school that day. Her neck was stiff and her head was pounding. When she tried to walk, she stumbled.

Dr. Kadel sent her to the hospital in Gettysburg. From there she was transferred to a larger facility in York. My mother prayed she would not have to be put in an iron lung.

The Health Department put a sign on our front door that we were contagious. *Quarantine: Do Not Enter*. I was very small, but I remember hearing the sound of them hammering the nails into the door.

Other men from the Health Department came for a home visit. They went into the pantry where we kids—there were six of us by then—washed our hands and faces and brushed our teeth at night. One of the men held up the toothbrush he'd taken from the glass jar beside the sink.

Had any of us used it?

No one answered.

Had we all used it?

My mother lowered her head in shame.

I was half-hidden behind the pantry door, but I remember that man, holding the toothbrush up for all to see, wanting an answer. I am haunted by it. I am haunted by the look on my mother's face.

There followed hard days.

Dad visited the local bank to ask for a loan.

They would consider. Come back in a week.

When there was no more coffee or sugar or flour in the house, my mother would take her list to the grocery store in Emmitsburg. Mr. Frailey, who owned the store, was kind enough to bag up her groceries and set them outside the back door for her to pick up. He didn't seem afraid of her.

The loan was granted, and Dad made plans to go to Canada to buy cattle certified free of tuberculosis and brucellosis. He rode a bus to Toronto where a cousin picked him up and drove him to a farm where there were cattle for sale.

Two weeks later, he came back, in the cab of a tractor trailer, twelve registered Holsteins loaded on the back. I remember two of them: Rag Apple and Queenie. Once, when Rag Apple was walking into her stall, she found a nest of kittens where she needed to put her feet. She used her nose to push them to the side, stepped forward, and put her head in the stanchion.

Rose came home, but she was unable to walk. The polio had affected her legs. In time, after much therapy, she improved.

There are other pictures on the wall in my living room. The sad old man is my great great grandfather. In 1863 he joined Lee's army, fought at Gettysburg and lost his leg.

My parents' wedding photo is there. They both lived well into their nineties. As did Mae and Rose. Bob did not.

Over the years the photograph of my family of origin has faded, but if you look closely, you can see that my father is holding Bob's hand. This is the son he yearned for.

My mother's hand is resting on Rose's shoulder.

Hans

B.A. Brittingham

He died on the Eastern front.

That's nearly all I know of him, this cousin named Hans.

He was the son of my grandmother's sister, Annalise, and I am certain that she mourned him with no less intensity than any other of the millions of soldier mommas did; even if he had fought for the deadly and dreadful Nazi regime.

These are among the things where a different level of humanity comes into play. Does the fact that one side of a war wins thus creating a defeated part really make any difference to those who suffer? It certainly exemplifies the terrible finales for those who choose to follow terrible leaders, even when they think they are selecting the right path for their country.

After World War I, the German people were financially and morally crushed by reparations forced upon them by the Allies who wanted to recover some of their massive military outlays. This was also intended to humiliate Germany and to fiscally cripple its economy so that they could not launch a comeback and another possible war.

We know how well that calculation turned out.

All nations are proud and self-important and perhaps the German Republic was a bit more. Stifled, starving, with high unemployment, they were stirred by the hollow promises of Adolph Hitler.

Where one lives has a heavy-duty influence on one's beliefs. My grandparents came to America in the early 1920s; they were too busy working to become standard Americans to pay much attention to the Nazi movement as it took seed in their homeland. When they did notice, there was a slight schism in family attitudes.

But by the mid-1930s, there were reports reaching the US of Hitler Youth Brigades, torch bearing night parades, and all the extreme measures invoked to terminate the Jewish population and thus solidify the public behind the deplorable burgeoning regime.

My grandmother once said, "I told my sister Annalise, if you follow Hitler, you will pay with your son."

And so, it came to pass.

Not only a soldier, Hans was also an SS member, in one of the most feared of Hitler's high ranking special cadres. These men were so devoted to their Führer that they blindly did anything he wanted regardless of its depravity. That was why Hitler sent them to the frontlines of newly occupied cities and countries: their grisly reputation preceded them forcing the conquered to timidly buckle under.

But Hitler's villainy was eventually short-circuited by the Russian army which had much more experience with fighting in the severe weather conditions of their own country.

I see this lost and distant cousin as he freezes to death, wondering in his still forming nineteen-year-old mind where the entire Nazi illusion went wrong. Did he live long enough to know that there were places like Auschwitz and Bergan-Belson? Was he aware of the Polish ghettos intended to exploit and convert to slave-labor (and eventual death) their occupants?

Probably not. And even if he did, what could he have done?

Whenever I think of him, he appears as a blond, blue-eyed figure wafting forth from a mist; or maybe the snowbank in which my fiction writer's imagination visualizes ice crystals forming in his blood as he perishes.

What do we do with such reprehensible images? All that youth, potential, and life pressed down into some great fatality pit alongside all those innocents — Jews and gypsies and Poles and Soviet POWs and Catholics and the mentally infirm and various dissidents. Etcetera.

Somehow the German population has found a way to deal with their appalling past which cannot be undone but must be accepted. It is called *Vergangenheitsaufarbeitung* and describes the attempt 'to analyze, digest and learn to live with the past, particularly the Holocaust.'

Don't all countries and populations have pasts with unspeakable portions to them; somewhere they slipped off the 'natural track' for whatever reasons? In our own nation, there are many: the forced importation of Africans, the genocide of our Indigenous People, the War Between the States, the incarceration of the Japanese during WW II. Much of the time it seems as though we handle these transgressions by sweeping them aside or going on with blinders affixed to our consciences.

Maybe it's all too difficult to look at, too many bodies, too much badness, too bleak an outcome. Maybe we need to remember it in terms of one, as the representative of the many.

When I think of Hans, I remember that like many of us, he was a victim of his time and political circumstance. That his death (and so many others) gave them (in some way) a quick relief from the sins of their community as a whole. It was left for the modern, mournful, and reflective nation to figure out how to process this tragic portion of history.

And yet, as we look towards the Middle East, we must wonder how they—and even our own national choices— will deal in the future with the steady climb of 41,000 plus deaths. Will there someday be an Islamic-Judeo *Vergangenheitsaufarbeitung?*

Or are we destined to never learn?

Niggling at Corners of the Mind

Mike Turner

She so loved life
The glory of a morning's sunrise
Bringing promise of the coming day
Learning a new fact
Re-reading a favorite book
Cherishing family
Making new friends

But something was niggling at the corners of her mind
Spinning cobwebs holding deep shadows
Drawing curtains of emptiness across her world

Slowly she began to forget
Numbers, words, phrases
Dates, places
Names, faces
Until now she sits
Day after day
In a "memory care facility"
Though she has little memory left to care for

Yet, still,
Each time I see her
She smiles

So loving life
Glorying in the morning sunshine
Anticipating what the new day will bring
Each fact learned afresh
Each story read for the first time
(Though I read to her, she having forgotten how)
Each person, a new friend

And when she looks in my eyes
Her countenance glows
As something niggles at the corners of her mind
She can sense it's there
Though she can't put a name to it
Or to me
And so she just smiles
And I remember
For both of us

Montecito

Leslie Zemeckis

There are three basic laws that the Chumash live by: *Limitation, Moderation and Compensation.* Limitation meaning our time on earth. Moderation, take from the land and ocean just what is needed, leaving food for future generations. Compensation, doing something for others because your heart tells you to, not for any gains. They leave by Nature's time, not man's, believing living by man's goes against the grain.

"We have to pay attention to the seasons, the changes of the land, the language of nature and the voices of its creatures. They give us insight about balance between us and our surroundings. They teach us respect for the plants that heal us and make our homes. The lessons teach us sustainability, and how to maintain our relationship with nature. It is a balance of survival."

Unfortunately, too often Man is oblivious or in denial of the consequences of his actions that are harmful to nature's system of life.

The unincorporated town of Montecito works hard to preserve its charming semi-rural character. There are no sidewalks, nor streetlights to break the darkness at night, which means the sky above is a galaxy of glittery stars. Horses can be heard cantering on narrow streets. The occasional mountain lion or bobcat hunts, scrawny coyotes roam in packs howling, hawks circle above. A black bear or two is spotted climbing fences, foraging from abundant fruit trees, or tearing into chicken coops. Grizzly bears were once abundant, foraging across the, then, densely wooded slopes.

January 9, 2018. In the early morning hours, the steep mountains above Montecito crumble, sending masses of boulders the size of SUVs, 70-foot trees building into giant twenty-five-foot waves of mud and debris, swooping up whatever lay in its path as it rushes towards thousands of sleeping residents.

The ensuing avalanche (technically plural as five events occur nearly simultaneously) grows like a yeasty ball of dough, higher and wider. Doubling. Tripling in size. Those who saw it - and lived - compared it to the movie "The Blob" as it absorbs, mashes, and crushes septic tanks, hot water heaters, washing machines, stoves, all bubbling up into a dense tsunami. Boulders bob the crest like marshmallows on frothing hot chocolate, massive tree trunks churn beneath, riding on mud and water at speeds of twenty-five miles per hour. The unsuspecting families sleeping below are exhausted after numerous evacuations from the Thomas Fire, which left the hills a slick surface unable to absorb the downpour of apocalyptic rain. They are sitting ducks.

In the days before, Christmas decorations had been packed away, trees discarded, tinsel and wrapping paper tossed. Sighs of relief echoed throughout the canyons; rain was on its way. The threat of fire was over. *No more evacuations*! Fire season came early this year. It is a lucky thing as there are no other conflagrations blazing anywhere in the country freeing eight thousand fire personnel to pour into Montecito and defend its roughly 8,600 residents. As flames licked dry hills, the sky blackened, but only seven structures would burn.

At 3:45 a.m. on January 9th, five major creeks (usually bone dry, because wasn't California always in a drought?) that cut through Montecito from the mountains to the ocean, filled and spilled when an unprecedented rain cell sat for five minutes directly over the new burn scar, dousing over half an inch of rain. Rain the mountain could not absorb.

Normally, rain would easily soak into the parched terrain. But the chaparral and scrub and plants holding the mountain together have a waxy coating, which has melted, leaving the mountain virtually waterproof. It is as if the mountain has donned a rain slicker.

Chaos ensues. A mother and daughter reach for each other, clasping hands as their house splits over their heads; a grandmother who has promised her son she would stay on the second floor, opens her front door and is yanked away. A father of six and one of his sons fight to keep their heads above the roaring water and debris that pulls them from their home that rips apart in seconds. One will die, the other will be found, naked, electrocuted from downed power lines, burnt, with multiple broken bones from boulders hitting him as he is swept a mile downhill, and dropped onto the 101 Freeway which fills with mud. A mother and her two young sons cling to a mattress as it lifts on a sea of mud and floats through a broken wall and out into the night. A pregnant woman crouches on a counter, watching as half her home washes away. Her husband and toddler in the side that disappears before her eyes. An elderly couple toss and turn as if they are a load of laundry in a giant washing machine, eyes filling with tiny rocks, certain they are going to die as they fight not to drown, calling each other's name. A brother just returned from a Brazilian vacation holds his sister in his arms while she bleeds to death in the pouring rain.

A town will wake to mass destruction, power outages, hundreds stranded, homes gone, hedges and lush gardens and acres of trees, now barren, mine-fields of rocks and mud. The sheriff will say it looks like a "war zone." Cars are mashed and twisted, strewn everywhere. Hundreds of them. Portions of homes hang in trees, like mangled toys. Bodies are buried under piles of debris, search dogs sniff for survivors. It will take six hours to pull a fourteen-year-old from the wreckage of her house, a pocket of air the size of a soccer ball the only thing keeping her from suffocating. A movie star and his wife hang on a wire above their mud-filled “forever” home, airlifted to safety, the wife, gripping a tiny old dog she refuses to leave behind. A son searches up and down the mud-drenched creeks in the following days, calling his mother’s name. Her body will be found near the beach.

The debris flow as it would become known would dominate headlines, talk shows and the 5 o’clock news for a few days then, as the news does, it moves on. Montecito becomes a blip in a fast-paced cycle of politics and other tragedies.

The Time of Leaving

Micah Ward

The air conditioner is an old window unit and struggles against an August night in Savannah. The man lies on the bed under a light film of sweat. The woman sleeps facing away and is covered to her waist by a sheet. He looks at the clock, 4:00 am. He might as well get up.

He walks quietly into the kitchen pulling on the old gym shorts he keeps by the bed. He doesn't want to wake the woman from her sleep. Earlier in the evening she had cooked a simple meal and afterwards they had enjoyed the comfortable loving of those who know they are past the exuberance of youth and are okay with it. He pours Tennessee whiskey silently. He knows that he shouldn't drink this close to leaving. But he has left so many times over the years that it has become something of a tradition.

He walks through the living room past the duffle bag and clothes. Opening the French doors, he steps outside onto the balcony which belongs to one of the four apartments in the 1940s era house. The sweat increases as he leans on the rail and looks at the sprawling live oak trees with their gray goatees of Spanish moss. It was hot in the Tennessee summers where he grew up. But this is wet blanket hot. A sticky hot that wraps around and weighs you down.

He looks down at his truck parked in the dirt parking area. The woman will keep it while he is gone. She will also close out the apartment and put his few possessions into storage. She's a better woman than most he has left and he wonders if he is a step up or a step down for her. She never talks about the other men. No complaining. No comparing. He is grateful for that.

He walks back into the apartment, cool now compared to outside on the balcony. He empties the last of the whiskey into his glass and crosses the living room. He sits in a chair, and looks at the duffle bag and the clothes on the sofa. He was twenty the first time he left and that was twenty-two years ago. There were more times of leaving between that first one and the one of this early morning. He might have avoided going this time if he spoke a quiet word to the right person. But something inside of him won't allow it. There are so many more stripes on his uniform now than there had been the first time. And more first timers going now that he feels responsible for. He considers waking the woman and trying to explain but he feels a lack of the proper words. It is hard to understand unless a person has been there or somewhere like it.

A soft light appears from the bedroom. He walks toward the kitchen and takes the last sip of his ceremonial whiskey. She walks from the bedroom wearing only a large gray tee shirt with ARMY written across the front. She makes coffee.

"You shouldn't have gotten up," he says.

"Is it time for you to leave?"

"Pretty close."

"I'll make you breakfast."

"You don't have to do that," he says and starts to dress in the living room.

"From the looks of that bottle you need something on your stomach."

He dresses amid the aroma of coffee and the sound of frying bacon. The same scene will repeat itself all over Savannah that morning and in most homes, it will be very ordinary, unlike the way it is here.

"I'll take you out to the base," she says, "I don't mind."

"I know you don't but I've already scheduled the taxi."

She brings two cups of coffee to the table. A plate with bacon, eggs, toast.

"It's not much but maybe it will get you to the next meal."

"Aren't you eating?"

"I'll have something later."

They sit in comfortable silence while he eats. When he comes back, they will have more quiet meals like this. And he will come back. He always comes back.

"I don't know when I'll get to call," he says. "It depends on the flight schedules and layovers."

"I understand. Call when you get a chance."

There is nothing else to say. They stand in the living room looking at each other. She places the green beret on his head. A hug. A brief kiss and he walks through the door with his duffle bag.

"I'll call as soon as I can."

"I'll be waiting."

He walks down the hall and she leans against the door frame and thinks of the last one. The one that did not come back.

Kudzu

John Drudge

Life runs thin
As a mountain stream
In late summer
Dwindling toward
Its inevitable end
Each drop mattering
Yet we squander
Spilling and hoarding
Pretending there is more
Than there is
Voices rising
Sharp and brittle
As frost on dry leaves
Each claiming the truth
While their roots
Rot in shallow soil
And the earth watches
Patient as we bicker
Over borders and doctrines
Drawing lines in the sand
That the tides will erase
Hypocrisy
Growing like kudzu
Choking wild spaces

While ideologies harden
Like old trails
Static and unyielding
Blind to the shifting path
In the wind
The endless sky
And the quiet rhythm
Of lone footsteps
On new dirt
Reminding us of what endures
And what does not

Mulberry Street to Dexter Avenue

Jennifer Susan Smith

Whitewash blood-soaked balcony,
on the motel's second story.
retrieve the misplaced necktie,
its knot ripped apart,
from walkway's concrete cold.
refashion its shattered print.
drape it around the collar of an
unstained dress shirt, white as
mourning florals edged in red.

Silence the sirens of Memphis.
restride through Room 306's door.
finish the ashtray's partial cigarette,
as smoke puffs dissipate bloodshed,
disguise hatred's horror. repack luggage
with first-year pastor's suits and sermons.
depart Mulberry Street, past Lorraine's
turquoise sign, skyward to Montgomery,
southeast, toward Dexter Avenue steeple.

How many miles must you fly to reach
the church by sunrise? How many steps
must you march to see spire reach sun?

stand in the Baptist pulpit, posture erect,
just after plane touches down, as arches
of colored glass windows admit morning
light, imbuing glory onto pews, engraining
their wood with a dream.

It's All For You

DeLane Phillips

Daddy says that if we want to see the Glory of the Lord we can't give You-Know-Who any room to dwell in our lives. He says that light can't abide with darkness in our house. So, Daddy told the Devil to leave the house. We can't even say his name, or the words "but," or "darn." We can't say the "devil" in the house, in a sentence, or anything. Mama made deviled eggs for lunch and we couldn't even say their names. Apparently they're stuffed now.

Daddy says we shouldn't even mention his name, the "you-know-who," because we'd be giving "you-know-who" the credit.

We gotta' give credit where credit's due, and that's to the Lort.

"What in the devil am I gonna do when my friends come over? How are we going to talk? They're sure not gonna' understand the difference between a devil and stuffed!" I demanded, stomping my foot, like Mama, with my hands on my hips.

Go to your room and don't come out! Daddy ordered. So, I did as I was told. From inside my room I listened to my parent's conversation. Daddy yelled at Mama,

She's gettin' too big fer 'ur britches, that little lady is!

The word of God says his name, so why can't I? For such a low-rotten, dirty fellow, this guy sure has a lot of names: devil, Satan, Lucifer, Evil One, and that's just a start. Mama calls my

Uncle Frank the Devil. Even the man of God yells his name every Sunday, while he preaches and sweats,

"Satan is like a roaring lion runnin' to and fro, seeking whom he may devour!" I've never seen a lion or a roaring one at that, but apparently the man of God ain't heard the ruckus my little brother makes. I heard Mama question Daddy.

What are you going to do when my brother visits?

My uncle smokes and Daddy won't allow him in the house. I held my breath, Don't you worry, I'll take care of him!

From my room at the door, I heard her let out a big sigh, and stomp her foot. I had to defend her.

"Why don't 'cha just move my little brother out then Daddy?" I stood in the kitchen, glaring at Daddy.

That would save Daddy and the Lord a whole 'lotta trouble. Then the Glory could move in and we'd all be happy I thought.

Go to 'ur room!

Again. I wanted to let out a big sigh and stomp my foot. I knew what would happen if I did. Being sent to a room is hard enough, but lying in the bed with a sore backside-not-but was worse.

I pouted all afternoon, mad as the You-Know-Who.

I know I'm not supposed to be mad. I'm saved and baptized. Getting' saved and baptized' was not as fun as I thought it would. I can't keep up with all the rules and I sure can't keep the "D" words from coming out my mouth.

In my room, lying on the bed watching my yellow rosy curtains flutter that Mama had sewn for me, I caught the smell of something sweet on the breeze. I sat up in bed and recognized the scent. It was my favorite dessert.

Mama opened the bedroom door and walked in. She was holding a large plate. Yer Daddy's gone down to the barn to feed the cows.

She smiled as if she knew a big secret. I peered out my bedroom window. Across the yard, through the garden and beyond, I could see Daddy walking along the path beside the pasture fence, with the cows following him towards the troughs for supper. I turned back and looked at Mama, smiling. She held a large plate in her hands. I inhaled the warm scent of chocolate.

The dark chocolate, sweet cake was still warm and fresh from the oven.

Smiling, Momna handed me the large plate. The slice of cake was big enough for two grown men to share! I thought I was dreaming. Speechless, I looked up at Mama, Well go on, it's all for you, she nodded.

The cake's frosting made my mouth water. I had watched Mama mix up batch after batch at the kitchen stove. I knew the recipe now almost by heart: the cocoa, butter, sugar, and vanilla. And for some reason, she always tossed in a pinch of salt.

The melted frosting dripped down the huge slice of cake onto the pretty plate. The plate was from Mama's special plates we only used for company! The fork was from her special box that contained all of the "family silver." I wasn't mad anymore. I was company! "What do I call it now Mama?"

Well, 'ur Uncle Frank calls it d' ….

"Stop, Mama!" I yelled.

Why?

"We can't say that word either."

What I Learned at the Opera

Julie Green

Richard's aria from *The Hours*, Act 2,
music by Kevin Puts, libretto by Greg Pierce

There is a story carried in music.
The man is dying. Someone always dies in opera.
In his hand he cradles a book, his sorrow
bleeding through the music as a last testament…

I wanted to make something true,
it didn't have to be great.

He clutches the book to his chest, weeping
that it be simply, good.
You don't have to be dying of aids to be there.
You don't have to be a writer to ride
the music into the scene as author, lover,
or the girl who might read it…

someone who is feeling hopeless.
someone you'll never meet.

You sit in the faceless gathering,
and each one bears a poem, drawing,
an impression, or unrealized thing.

It doesn't have to be great, this work
for someone you may never know to see
and take it into the parched hollows
of their heart.

The writer grips the book and moves
to the open window…

*Maybe, just maybe it will keep her alive long
enough to write a poem for someone else.*

The music stills, suspending us there.

We prowl through rooms, the dry cleaners,
a school, an office park. The cost of survival
is to make, and the need seeps into the air.

As he falls from the window, we are the man,
our music simmering along a tender line
that stutters, groping for contact with the hopeless girl.

She is always here in the crowd,
around, and within us.

Nobody
(For those battling)

Ann Hite

Nobody likes to talk about your feelings.
Push them down, step away.
No one wants to hear your heart spilling
All over the page. Not really.

Nobody likes to hear about your challenges. Not really.
They smile. They nod when they are supposed to.
They step away to other thoughts. Their thoughts.
Your heart rips in half when you can't help those struggling.

Nobody likes to talk about the hard edges inside your life, hidden
In the shadows. Not really. No one wants to reach out for long.
Hurry and get better. Speed it up. Often they don't think outside themselves.
Not for long. They nod when they are supposed to.
Until they don't hear anymore.

Nobody likes to hear about the crumbling dream.
Move on. Don't stay there.
Won't that feel better? Not really.

They refuse to see your feet sunk in hardening cement. No one cares
To see, to feel, the deep, deep struggle and emotions.

Nobody likes to hear about your successes. Not really.
Unless the winning moment reflects them. No one understands the distance
To cover between pain and happiness. Nobody sees the tears flooding a
Broken heart. Not really.

Nobody likes to talk about the inability to cope with stress built around you
A wall high and long like the Great Wall of China.
No one hears the whispers in your heart.
The empty space, the ripple of breaking glass. Not really.

Nobody wants to hear you tell them no, telling them it is too much,
Too hard, too long. They hate the word too. Shadows fall around you.
Working around your shoulders, a heavy cloak on the shoulders

Of each nobody who turns away to see their reflections in the glass of water. Not really.

Nobody wants to talk about you crying out in pain. The process is too hard.
All you know is what lives around you. The heart of the story and life
Worth living, worth chasing, worth fighting for.
The process is too hard. Not really.

The Deception of Hester Prynne

Mary Kendall

Hester Prynne picked her way through the woods, traveling deeper to forage for wild wine berries. Those with the deepest, richest flavor grew abundant in a glade bathed in sunlight, just beyond a small pond.

The trail opened up with the clearing where she paused to lift her heavy, dark mane from her neck. She tied its weight into a knot and swept it off to one side. As she felt a light pulse of cool air, a reprieve from the humid summer day, she caught sight of the ruby red color that ringed the tranquil space, the berries. But Hester stopped short before entering; she did not have it to herself.

In the very middle, a visitor sat perched on the edge of a stump. She recognized his shining crown of gold hair from her vantage. The young minister recently assigned to head up King's Chapel and guide the villagers on their spiritual paths was a beautiful specimen of a man.

Upon first clapping eyes on Arthur Dimmesdale, she had thought of none other. Now, he appeared in deep reverie, gazing above at the bright, blue sky. She hesitated no more and walked forth with determination.

A few feet apart, his eyes, depths of dark pitch, studied her. She closed the gap and reached over to touch his delicate features that filled with amazement at her bold action. She traipsed fingers along his neck, down his chest, then lower. He made a sound of protest but she pressed on until he protested no more.

Their coupling was a frenzy of friction on the floor of the glade. It also led to a piece of grit between them that was enough to bind. In time, it would become a pearl. Her Pearl.

Later, he said, "I have lost my mind. Hellfire will come upon us both." She shushed him with her mouth.

Summer drew to a close. The woods became sparse of foliage, no longer a safe meeting place from peering village eyes. The lovers were left with secretive and strangled glances exchanged at church services and occasional village functions.

In time, Hester discovered trysts in the glade had resulted in her belly and breasts becoming full. She knew what was coming and disguised it through her clothing selections, generous and billowing.

Her husband, much older than her, had left several years earlier to travel overseas for scholarly endeavors. She had awaited his return in their thatched roof cottage on the far edge of the village, but no one had received word of him. She hoped he would not return in fact. The selectmen allowed Hester to remain in the cottage, on her own, as she took good care of it.

She now had every intention to protect Arthur and his position as the Bay Colony's spiritual director. She would not reveal the nature of their relationship—until he was ready. Tethered by his responsibilities and duties, she assumed they might go elsewhere to make a life once his appointment was complete.

With each passing month, her size became greater and more unwieldy with trips into the village increasingly difficult. As the time grew near, she squirrelled away provisions necessary for her confinement and then stayed put, hoping to be left alone.

Thanks to her attendance at many births, Hester knew what to do. She kept a clear head and birthed by herself; floundering at points, but making it through. Afterwards, she nursed both herself and the infant on her own. But, within a short time period, a goodwife arrived at her doorstep seeking herbs and heard the infant's cries.

Word got out about Hester's secret, a baby but no husband at her cottage near the woods. Soon after, she found a letter staked to her door decreeing mandatory attendance at the next selectmen's meeting.

On the appointed day, she closed up the cottage and slowly walked to the village with her babe, Pearl, strapped to her bodice. She gazed down atop her infant's head, incredulous still such a miracle had come to her.

She moved with caution on the path strewn with broken twigs and branches, winter's residuals. Two months after the birth, her body tinged and ached in places, not yet back to what it had been. Still, it was good to be outside after little activity.

As she neared town, furls of smoke rose from chimneys in cottages sprinkled along the path. At the top of the main street, she remembered it was market day seeing more hustle and bustle and people afoot. She considered some purchases after the meeting, after whatever was to occur.

She passed the blacksmith's shop with its open bay and he gazed at her, unsmiling, face black with soot. Further along, several goodwives standing by the cooper's shop stopped talking as she passed. She gave a nod getting none in return, only a flicker of compassion on one of the faces. News of her baby had filtered throughout town.

As she crossed paths with others and experienced similar reactions, the walk to the meeting house became never-ending. She stumbled at one point and barely caught herself, hearing a snicker but pressing on. The harbor, laying off to one side, water shimmering from bright sunlight, offered an escape someday if these reactions were to be her life.

Finally, the meeting house stood in front of Hester, a wood frame building imposing in stature. She pulled herself up the three tall steps to the entrance, short on breath once at the top. She shook herself, dismayed by this sign of weakness.

She opened the door and entered the wide, open-spaced room with its roughhewn rafters exposed as the ceiling. A table dominated the center, where a handful of men, the selectmen, the pillars of the community as it were, sat. They were a blur of sameness to Hester in their puffed white collars, dark attire, thin beards and gray hair.

None rose as a sign of respect, their expressions censorious. She felt a sinking sensation at being cast and judged as a fallen woman. As she steeled herself, Pearl made a mewing sound. All eyes moved to where the baby was bound on Hester's bodice.

Pearl bore a striking beauty even to a casual observer. She already had a full mane of golden hair, her father's color. But her facial features were her mother's; big, brown eyes, a button of a nose and rosebud lips.

Goodman Billings stood up at the head of the table and cleared his throat. "Mistress Prynne. Please sit," gesturing to a vacant spot.

Once she was seated, he spoke again. "So, we will commence. It has come to the selectmen's attention that you have conducted relations outside of the marital contract. The result being the babe in your arms."

Hester said nothing nor did the other men around the table. She glanced around in the brief silence taking stock. There was an unease with where the proceedings would be taking them.

She knew all of the men. Their wives utilized Hester's skills to keep their husbands' attire in a fitting manner. Hester's seamstress talents made the ruffles in their collars so precise and perfect. Hester was compensated with pittances that kept her and her flock of chickens fed with enough also to maintain her dwelling if needs arose.

Goodman Billings made an overt noise in his throat then continued. "We demand now that you tell us the father of the infant so proper steps can be taken." It was unspoken what those steps would be. Prior history of punishments in the community did not preclude hanging on the scaffold in the village square.

Hester blinked, then spoke one word. "No."

There was a collective and uncomfortable shuffle around the table. Billings looked around for someone else to jump in but no one did. His voice came out in a fiercer tone. "Mistress, you will tell us or else…or else you will be confined to the stockade."

A laugh burbled up from somewhere deep within. It came out sounding like anything but merriment. "Do as you must."

Hester sat down heavily onto the thin, musty pallet; Pearl, asleep on her chest. She let out a sigh and eyed up the porcelain bowl in the corner for toilet needs. The barest sniff of fresh air along with a glimmer of light filtered through a slit in the wall. Her punishment was a set period of days confined to the stockade cell.

There was one other item; materials for embroidery. Fine red thread and gold cloth lay at the end of the pallet along with an open case of several sewing needles made from animal bones. Whilst jailed, she had been instructed to sew the letter A to be affixed to her garments. Hester's skills, known throughout the village, were now to be used against her as she was tasked to stitch her own sentence. A for Adulteress.

Hester picked up thread, spooling out some through her fingers. What no one realized was her prowess went beyond just expert embroidery. She let out a mirthless laugh over the village gossips, prideful and puffed up with suspicions. But ignorant about who really dabbled in witchcraft amongst them. In fact, her stitchery could easily become witchery.

Days in the cell passed much the same with the most meagre of provisions given twice daily; a broth long gone cold, a hunk of stale bread and a vat of water. She felt herself becoming lighter in weight and could only hope the rations would sustain her nursing of Pearl.

Pearl was a good sleeper so, when not tending to her, Hester perfected the letter's stitching on its backdrop of gold-colored cloth. At one point, she begged for additional spools saying it did not stand out enough. Granted her request, she used it for her own intents and purposes, not theirs. Even though light was dim, the startling effect was evident as she pulled strands back and forth. No spool of thread was ever dyed the exact same hue so different red tones worked in her favor.

While village folk relied on her sewing and herbal remedies, they knew nothing of her calling upon ancestral spirits for a spell or an incantation. Now, she depended upon those spirits to craft her punishment, the letter A. She had to be careful though. Mistress Hibbins was presently under fierce scrutiny on trumped up accusations of witchcraft. The specter of the gallows loomed ahead of any woman suspected of tangling in the dark arts. But that gossip had never been pinned on Hester.

Time in the chilly, dank cell passed by in this manner until the end result pleased Hester—greatly. When her sentence was up, they were brought out from the cell to outdoors where she and Pearl blinked their eyes like moles emerging from underground.

After being led to the meeting house, Hester found herself again surrounded by the selectmen at the table. This time, however, Hester wore the Scarlet A across her bodice. She lifted Pearl up before she sat down. All of them got an eyeful of the letter that shimmered and danced and they reeled back from the sight.

What exactly were they viewing? What they had mandated yet not as expected, it was…it was…exquisite artwork. The letter was defined in a way that twirled in front of their view. Was it even really an A? One could almost make out other letters within it…a P, a H, a M….it was almost magical but magic was against all Puritan teachings. It had to be just an A. Their minds settled on that deeming it so.

As Goodman Billings gave her the slimmest smile, Hester noted his eyes, an icy blue, not unlike those of her missing husband. "Well, it is evident you made use of your time to embroider the A. Now, you can still change all of this and tell us the name of the man."

Just as before, Hester repeated, "No."

He cleared his throat. "If that is your decision, this board condemns you to wearing the Scarlet Letter at all times from this point forward."

Hester made her way over the uneven landscape, balancing her strapped-on babe with a basket of goods to sell in the village, her first venture back since released from the stockade. The cold nip still in the air reminded it was imperative to get provisions from the local shops. But her main objective for the trip was to come face to face with him. She had been patient long enough. It was time.

As Hester neared town, she crossed paths with Goody Johnson, an ancient lady who tottered around with the aid of a cane carved out of birch. The woman eyed her under her heavy, white-haired brows. "The nerve of you, coming to town, bold as can be." She spat in front of Hester's boots.

Hester lifted Pearl away from her chest to expose the Scarlet A. The woman took a faltering step back, almost falling over. She sputtered out, "It's evil you are. I don't know what I even look at." She averted her gaze from the sight as if blinded.

Heartened at the letter's effect, Hester put Pearl back in place, covering the A, and walked on. Her presence in town drew out small groups to gawk. Most gave a wide berth and cast their eyes to the side, preferable to Goody Johnson's reaction.

She pulled herself up, tall and proud, continuing to her destination, undeterred. She let the loud and pretend whispers, vicious in intent, waft over her. "Look at her brazenness walking right towards chapel" and "Our poor reverend having to contend with her type."

She reached the chapel, located diagonal from the harbor's edge, where she expected Arthur inside at midday in his offices. A cluster of gossips with the most clout stood in front and stared her down, blocking her entry.

She took them in as a collective, all clothed in gray woolen cloaks that bespoke of their standing in the village hierarchy. Some were the very same who employed her to stitch their husbands' garments which counted for nothing now by their tally.

One spoke up. "Not seemly to walk into the house of the Lord with such a stain on your person, indeed on your soul." Hester lifted her baby just enough for the letter to be shown. The gossips, struck silent, turned their gazes away.

As they stepped aside, she made her way to the rear door. After knocking, she heard the voice that had whispered tender sweet nothings into her ear on so many summer afternoons speak, "Enter."

She pushed the door open and stood on the threshold. He looked over from where he sat at the desk with a quill pen and rag paper. He immediately paled at the sight of her and the baby, his baby.

"Hester…" His voice came out in a falter.

Without invitation, she walked into the small room and sat across from him. It had all been worth it, the imprisonment in the stockade and the village's shaming, because Arthur would do right by them. "Aye. I am here." He was without words, mouth gaped open.

"Arthur. The time is nigh. Time that we are a family, the three of us. My husband is presumed lost at sea. We can approach the selectmen and be betrothed. Or we can just leave. Tell no one anything."

She adjusted Pearl to lay along her lap, the letter on her bodice in full reveal. His dark eyes nearly popped out at the sight. "Hester, what am I viewing? What is this?"

She stared down her nose at it, her handiwork. "It's rather beautiful, isn't it?

He stuttered. "But…but…it was supposed to be your punishment."

She cocked her head at him. "MY punishment?"

"Yes, yes for…" His voice trailed off as his gaze took in the slumbering babe.

"Pearl is not a punishment. She is the most amazing gift that could ever be bestowed upon me…upon us."

The couple was silent, Arthur's eyes not meeting hers.

"So…it is time." Hester repeated herself.

He cleared his throat and finally looked up to face her. "I cannot do as you ask, Hester. My vocation makes that an impossibility."

"Your vocation?"

"Yes. All of my years of learning at Oxford and devoting myself to procuring a position such of this one…I…I cannot abandon that."

She swallowed and then said, "But… I thought…when the time was right…when you were ready…"

He nervously clenched and unclenched his fists. She noted a show of perspiration on his upper lip. "Is the child even mine?" he said in a soft voice.

She reeled back, the impact as if he had physically hit her. "How dare you! After I withstood all of this, thinking you were of the same mind."

She stopped talking with sudden realization. The man in front of her, the man she had given her heart to, was a coward. He had sat by and let her suffer and be punished for months with no consequence for himself.

Arthur went even paler under her appraising gaze. Then he stood up. "I need to usher you out, Hester. The gossips will take note and—"

She put up a hand. "Stop your words."

Her internal emotions were in a rapid boil. Before they could overflow, she stood, lifting Pearl and rising up into that somewhat ungainly shape of mother and child, bound together.

As Hester stared at Dimmesdale, the thought occurred that this was the moment of her awakening. She was a woman scorned....and there would be a reckoning. She turned and took her leave.

Hester waited until all were at Sunday service thus leaving her path free from any encounters. Arriving at the chapel, she knew all were seated, filling the pews, as the service commenced a quarter of an hour earlier. She took a deep breath and gazed down into Pearl's eyes, eyes that stared back with complete adoration.

She hesitated for just a beat then flung the double wooden doors wide open. They made a screeching sound followed by the thud of hitting sidewalls. Dimmesdale, facing his flock in the middle of an exhortation, was the first to see her before all others turned back at the noise. He stopped mid-sentence and fell silent.

Never once had Hester presented any disorder to the village. Instead, she had been a model citizen—with the one exception that led to her lettered bodice. But now creating disorder was a must. She strode down the center before any officiant could even think to act, barely aware of the audible gasps echoing through the cold and airless room.

In front of the congregation, she stepped up to stand by Dimmesdale's side at the altar. She grabbed his arm covered by the flowing vestment and announced, "I am ready to reveal the father of my baby." He did not resist as she raised his limp arm up high. Her words dripped with scorn and bitterness she now felt for her erstwhile lover. "The great Reverend Mister Arthur Dimmesdale."

Goodman Billings sprang up from his front row seat. "This is preposterous! Mistress Prynne, I command you to step down at once!"

A low buzz of outrage had started up in pews. The noise became loud with some crying out, "Take her away! Take her to the gallows!" Several joined Billings, moving in force towards the altar.

Dimmesdale had gone mute, pounding on his heart with a free hand with the other still raised up by Hester. She released her hold on Dimmesdale and swiftly placed Pearl at her feet. Standing up tall, the Scarlet A blazed brighter than ever. The men faltered in their movements giving her the moment needed.

Her voice, strong and clear, yelled out, "Let me prove it!"

In the pause of the men paralyzed and still, she picked up Pearl and removed the loose-fitting red gown. Pearl gave a little screech of complaint at cold air striking her bare torso. Shushing Pearl's cries, Hester turned the baby outwards to face the congregation now in rapt attention.

She held out the side of Pearl's little body where sat a most unusual birthmark. It appeared as large, strawberry-colored and slightly raised in an arc shape, like a sickle seen out in the fields. Arthur had never held the babe, much less showed any interest in examining her, thus he was ignorant of this tell-tale sign. But now it was Hester's currency.

Goodman Billings spoke in the harshest of reprimanding tones. "Mistress, this proves nothing. Now come down here right now and—"

Hester cut him off. "Dimmesdale has the exact same."

"That's enough! You will speak no more nonsense in this sacred space—"

Goodman Parker stepped forward and cut off Billings saying, "I say Dimmesdale can settle this once and for all by lifting his vestment." He then glared at Dimmesdale with suspicion as Hester's ploy took hold.

"No! Of course, the Reverend will not be made to do that!"

The congregation began to talk aloud; some crying out that Hester needed to be taken away, others calling out for Dimmesdale to prove otherwise. Goodman Billings put a hand up to halt all the noise. "We shall put it to a vote."

He waited for the room to quiet down. "All in favor, raise a hand." Raised hands filled the room, a clear majority with curiosity winning over decorum.

Dimmesdale stepped down from the altar with a heavy tread, away from Hester and Pearl. He spoke for the first time since Hester's dramatic entrance. "There is no need." He paused, gathering strength, then said, "I fathered the babe."

The room erupted in chaos. A cacophony of outrage fired up with people standing and yelling in angry voices about Dimmesdale and his fate. Hester took the opportunity to scoop up Pearl and escape out the sacristy door. She needed nothing more from Dimmesdale or the village.

Running with Pearl to the nearby harbor, Hester's mind went back to her cottage that morning where she had chosen straightforward deception for her revenge instead of witchery. While Pearl slept deeply, Hester had dipped her blunt-edged bone needle into wine berry liquid, saved from summer's harvest and thickened with root flour. The needle tickled Pearl just enough that she let out a small sigh. Hester had stood back, needle in hand, to let the babe settle. Then she painted the design etched so well in memory, Arthur's birthmark.

After each pass dried, Hester applied layers until they stippled atop Pearl's smooth, dewy, alabaster skin and resembled Arthur's mark. After she finished the artistry, she had thought to herself, not for the first time, that red really was a magnificent color. When it was time to leave for the service, she clothed Pearl in the loose-fitting red gown to disguise any berry paint rubbing away.

Now, she relished the sight of the Victory in the harbor, the ship departing to parts southern. The day prior, she had arranged passage with the captain for the destination where she and Pearl would find a home. A sailor, casting ropes back to the dock, called out in a sing-song manner, "All aboard who are going aboard!"

Hester grabbed her clutch bag, hidden under a canvas earlier, that held all her modest possessions. The sailor lent her a hand, saying, "Almost too late, Mistress. Hop up." They were aboard seconds before the Victory drew away from the harbor.

A buzz in the distance came from church members as they got closer. Someone spotted her on the ship and yelled out, "There she is!"

Hester moved to the Victory's aft. Once enough witnesses had gathered, she brutally wrenched off the Scarlet A and hurled it into the open air. The letter arced over the churning waters, twisting and sparking with a life of its own; something apart from Hester, something apart from all things.

It landed on top of the water without even a hint of a splash. All fixated on the Scarlet A dancing and springing along with the swift current, venturing off to a place unknown, eventually to be pulled under and away forever.

Mimi and Bess

John M. Williams

In "my" china cabinet sits a porcelain cheese server, a misshapen, florid curiosity with a lid, as it has in blissful obscurity for twenty-something years. The only reason you're reading this story is because, as I was retrieving something from that antique cavity a few days ago, it caught my eye and fired a buried memory neuron.

I have only a few fragments of what might be called fact in this tale, and as you might guess, there's no one now to ask. I confess that some of what follows may be invented. Memory, invention—what's the difference? The main character, Mimi, my paternal grandmother, and her cruelladevillean older sister, Bess, are long gone. But in their childhood they would have been familiar with that piece of dishware which their mother, my great-grandmother Miss Ida, who lived to be 106, brought out only at Christmas.

To my way of thinking, there wasn't much worth grasping among Miss Ida's worldly goods, there being no money and hence no will, only some household items and an heirloom or two—the aforementioned china cabinet, an antique Philco phonograph with a cache of 78s, a clattery chandelier, and so on—and it may have been that scarcity which gave to a random piece of crockery such potential meaning. That meaning came to fruition when Miss Ida died, and the grasping began.

Actually it began some weeks before the actual event, when its inevitability became clear.

The sisters, as sisters will, had fought from the crib up, battles which Bess usually won. She had no soul and the tenacity of a pit bull and would have been a ruthless businesswoman except that she lived in the south in an age when women didn't have careers, unless squeezing the blood out of her turnip husband Elmer counts as one. So in this case you can imagine to which Cadillac-driving sister the choicest pieces of Miss Ida's estate went.

Except for the cheese server.

On that point, Mimi stood her ground. I'm pretty sure the dish meant nothing, really, to her, and that this fight was not about an object at all, but one fueled by spite, envy, the will to power, and the need for at least a minor victory every now and then.

"I will *have* that dish!" Bess, unrivaled in having, vowed.

But somehow Mimi ended up with it, keeping it under lock and key, and vowing to have it interred with her if she died first.

Which she did.

"I'll get it out!" Bess had sworn.

Which she did. At the Visitation.

She waited until the modest crowd of bereaved had thinned, then slipped into the Viewing Room where one of the ghoulish and promising young assistant funeral directors caught her up to her shoulders in the casket. "Adjusting her dress," she claimed.

"Mam, I assure you we have made every effort to—"

"Why don't you make an effort to get the hell out of here so I can have some quality time with my departed sister," Bess overpowered him—and then, almost tipping the casket, in her dear sister's lap—*found it!*

I can easily imagine the triumphant gleam in her eye, the rich gratification coursing through her blood, even perhaps a little Hitlerian jig of conquest, there in that hushed room, holding the dish over her head like a rival's severed head.

I don't know how these emotions fared over the three years she outlived Mimi—I like to think they lost *some* of their glow—but die indeed she did, and no one mourned.

In the dispensing of *her* effects, she had outlived everybody who might have wanted any of them, which I'm betting was nobody, and certainly not Mama. Daddy, who liked to fish, couldn't have cared less.

And that's how I, the unlikeliest of beneficiaries, ended up with the cabinet and its collection of curios, including an ornate and forgotten cheese server, dusty and ridiculous.

Why I Said What I Said to the Bartender

Alaina Hammond

You are six years old. I referred to you—in the presence of the bartender and no one else—as a fucking cunt.

My exact words were "I hate that fucking cunt."

And this is what I meant by that.

I said I hate you, because I find it frustrating that you so consistently steal time from your classmates, while compromising their learning. I'm annoyed that you deliberately monopolize our attention by acting out. Camilla can barely read, but she's quiet. Thus our eyes are on you, instead of on Camilla, who surely needs them more.

Frankly, I resent the way the other teachers reward you for your bad behavior. They feed your vicious cycles with their indulgence. As the teacher with the least authority, I'm in no position to tell them that. And I'm annoyed at you for creating that hidden schism between myself and the colleagues I otherwise respect.

I said I hate you, but what I mean is that I'm disturbed by your bursts of violence. I have a bruise on my hand from when I blocked your blows, directed at Matthew. The book you used was sharp and heavy, which was why you chose to hit him with it. Also, you hurt my head when you threw a pencil at me, on purpose, because you didn't want to do math. And in that moment, yes, I hated you. You're vicious. You're feral. You suck.

I told the bartender I hate you because I can't tell YOU that. I have to take your shit, because it's my job. It's exhausting having to constantly censor myself all the time. So I said it to the bartender instead, because that way you don't have to deal with my anger. By letting off steam in that moment I can find the strength to do this shit again next week. Letting myself insult you, uncensored, is part of the process in which I stay kind to you.

I called you a cunt, and I said that I hate you, because I've seen the way your parents and your grandparents are with you. How loving, how patient, how involved in your education all four of them are. You seem to have no respect for the depth of your good fortune. You literally spit on your beleaguered mother, when she said it was time for you to leave. You fucking cunt, what a cunty thing to do!

I called you a cunt and said I hate you because you made fun of Emily's weight the other day. At six, you know damn well how cruel you're being.

I called you a cunt because you WORRY me. I'm worried about your future. I'm worried that your impulse control issues will only increase as you get older. I'm worried that these problems will avalanche into academic challenges you can never overcome. I'm worried that you will never achieve your potential.

I said I hated you because I've seen what you're capable of, when you apply yourself. And what I hate is the idea that you'll squander your natural talent. Already, you're behind where I think you could be, if you tried even a little bit harder.

I said I hate you because while I recognize that there are parts of your brain that are completely outside of your control, I also see you as having a great deal of agency. I see you as a full person, and not a blank victim, defined exclusively by what's wrong with you. You are not a marionette, controlled by your learning disabilities. I said I hate you, because I hate the choices you make.

I said I hate you because, after having known you merely two months, I fucking love you, as I love all your classmates who aren't a constant pain in my ass. I hate that you have that much power over me, that you have forced me to care about you as much as I do. It's annoying. You're annoying. Fuck you.

Today you gave me a card with my name on it. You signed your name with hearts.

Then later, when I told you not to look at Sophia's paper, you screamed at the top of your lungs. But you then stopped looking at Sophia's paper, which means I'm making progress with you. A few weeks ago, you might have thrown your chair across the room, so enraged at being told what to do. Instead, you merely vocally expressed your displeasure—LOUDLY—then concentrated on your own work. The scream was part of your emotional self-regulating process.

Also, you screamed because you're an obnoxious little cunt.

I showed the bartender the card you made me. He recognized your name, and he asked me, is that the cunt?

Yes, I told him. That's the cunt.

I'm putting it on my fridge.

Cunt.

Ode on Individualism's Twentieth Century Trinity of Champions
(an Acrostic)

Jake Sheff

"If I know your sect, I anticipate your argument."
Ralph Waldo Emerson, Self-Reliance

Ever the scientist, all you dreamt
Invented the void, like a Gustav Klimt.
Nazi Germany's oodles of plans
Surrounded the absence for which it stood.
Then its loneliest sect of one, you stood
Erect on that emptiness. (Now, it shines
In perpetuity.) Lit by your saber,
Nihility's time's unlovable neighbor.

II.

Assumptions begat so much, but your lines
Undid the most colorable of them all.
Dexterity's fall into disrepair
Engendered despair, then you banged your tabor…
Nullity's no unlovable neighbor.

III.

Agita aimed at the general will
Reveals nothingness ten times more than fear
Ever could. But you had arousal's ear…
No wonder a womb's-worth of knowledge fell
Despondently after you tossed your caber.
Titillation's awe's unlovable neighbor.

Weren't We Beautiful

(A tribute to the women in my family)

Ann Hite

Weren't we beautiful in the morning, waiting for the bus. The sun still far from showing itself, the day the black cloud rolled through the sky, turning the air yellow and green, splitting the place with a bolt of lightning, crackling in our hair and leaves of the trees, whipping in a frenzy over the moment of change.

Weren't we beautiful in the heart of the country dirt roads, gravel spraying us when cars drove by. Flowers dotting the forest floor, the wild blueberry bushes, the thorny blackberries, pulling at our tender skin, staining our fingers with purple juice.

Weren't we beautiful watching the mountains in the distance colored in orange, yellow, and red. The source of water flowing to the sea, to the place where we camped in pup tents. The raccoons gathering on the edge of the darkness, waiting for us to drop a crumb. The ocean moving in and out, shifting under our feet, sifting the sand like flour sprinkling in a big bowl like snow falling outside the window.

Weren't we beautiful in the warmth of a fire on a freezing night, cracking and popping with sparks escaping the stove door, heat dancing through the cold house, taking off the edge.

Weren't we beautiful in blouses covered in little sequins, the gray of our hair turning snow white. The heart of the holiday most loved. Toys and lights. Banana bread and sugar cookies with green and red icing. Knights and horses with bows and arrows surrounding the castle.

Weren't we beautiful walking in the mountains, a place that filled our hearts with long ago happiness, the clean crisp air, the bright blue sky. Trees scrubbing the clouds, catching them, pushing them to the ground.

Weren't we beautiful scrub boards in hand, washing clothes, hanging them on the line outside. Clothespins gripping the edges as wind whipped them straight into the air.

The Golden Locket

JoyAnne O'Donnell

From the rising gold leaves
Inside my locket of joy
Gold that is mine
Forever in my heart and mind
When memories are so kind
Time of great laughs
Time to remember
Music playing
Seeing harmony
The key to keep around my neck
Close to my heart forever
My souls chime
To be one with time
From the golden light
Beams my hearts sunshine
Inside my golden heart's locket
A walk to remember on the beaches rhyme
The waves flow thoughts so glowing
Blue sky so warm
The sand so soft
Dreams to come
To see engraved in my locket's true sparkle
with time.

Merle

Aaron Goodman

Someone knocked on our door. It was late.

I lay still. I knew my mother heard it. She'd come home after weeks in the hospital. My mom said she had a nervous breakdown. A doctor told my father it was manic depression.

Again, knuckles on wood. My mother got up and walked down the stairs.

My dad wasn't home. He was a firefighter and started picking up extra shifts when my mom got sick. Most days, he left the house before dawn and came back when I was asleep.

I sat on the steps. My mom opened the door and cold air blew around my legs. A man stood outside. I couldn't see above his belt from where I was. A tweed overcoat came to his knees and a duffel bag lay next to his leather boots.

"You're kidding," my mother exclaimed and put her arms around him.

She reached for his bag, but he got hold of it first. I glimpsed his white cheeks, overgrown moustache, and tired eyes beneath a brown fedora. It was my grandfather.

My mom backed up. He came in and put his bag down. Then he knocked his boot heels on the floor, removing a dusting of snow.

"You left the west coast for this?" my grandpa said and feigned a shiver.

"It's January, Dad."

It was a decade since we'd seen my grandfather. There weren't any phone calls. No letters or cards. The last time we were together, I was four, and we pulled away from our house in East Vancouver to move to Ottawa. My parents put suitcases in the back of their station wagon. I was crammed in with our stuff. I turned to see my grandfather, standing in front of our house, biting his lip.

When we lived in Vancouver, Grandpa Merle's place wasn't far from ours, but he rarely came by. Once my mom and I met him at a movie theatre. They got into an argument before the film began, and he emptied a box of popcorn on her shoes.

My grandfather put a hand on the wall and pulled off his boots while my mother held his hat. I looked at his hair, grey and oily with comb tracks in it. He was handsome but worn-looking like Errol Flynn near the end of his life.

My grandpa moved to the round wooden table that my mom got at the Stittsville Flea Market and pulled out a chair. I stood behind my mother as he rubbed his temples.

"Three days on a Greyhound, Evie," he said. "Can door flapping open the whole time."

"You didn't think of calling?" she said.

"I came because I heard you were in trouble," he replied.

How did he know?

My grandfather leaned a hand on the table and stood up. Then he looked at me for the first time.

"Trying to hide, hey?" he said.

"I'm not hiding," I answered.

"Hug your grandfather and go back to bed," my mom told me.

"Don't be a stranger," he said.

My mother poured him some milk.

"You know, I'm lactose intolerant," he said, eyebrows cinched together.

My mom put the bagged milk in its plastic holder back in the fridge.

"I'll put a foamie on the floor in Aziel's room for you," she said, gripping the refrigerator door handle.

The house was ripe with his body odour, the smell of the bus, and he was going to sleep next to me?

I was in bed and my grandfather dragged his bag up the stairs. It slumped on each step. He let it flop on the floor at the foot of the foamie my mom set down. Then he took off his pants, draping them over the back of my desk chair. His belt buckle knocked against the wood. He got on his knees in his boxers and undershirt, fumbled for the blanket, and lay down.

I woke to the sound of him ruffling under the covers. It was nearly midnight and he kept going. My eyes felt heavy, the bedroom cramped. I imagined my dad's face in the morning when he'd see Grandpa Merle.

A few years earlier, my mom considered calling her father. "Forget it," my dad said. "He's a used car salesman."

My grandfather restored early-century cars. My dad had other reasons for disliking him. He abandoned my mom when she was a girl after her mother died. And before my parents got married, he said my father was a "Jew boy."

I spun around in my bed, shut my eyes, and felt ill. Was he cranking himself?

My father came up the stairs. He was home from his shift. I turned and he was fixed on my grandfather.

"Jesus, Merle," my dad said.

***

In the morning, my grandpa was in the bathroom, water running in the sink, but it was otherwise quiet. He didn't come out for a long time.

"Dad?" my mother said at the door.

My grandfather emerged holding a razor blade cartridge in one hand, a handle in the other. His expression was blank. My grandpa was sixty-something and forgot how to shave?

In the kitchen, my mother beat eggs with a fork and poured them over onions and mushrooms in her cast iron pan. My grandfather, smelling like aftershave, announced he was going to make verenekies, and that I'd help.

He searched the cupboards, pulling out my mom's Five Roses flour and measuring spoons.

"Just tell me what you need," my mother said.

"You don't remember?" my grandpa asked. "How many times did we make verenekies when you were a girl?"

She pushed her tongue into her cheek. It's one thing to ditch a child, another to pretend it didn't happen.

"Verenekies?" I said.

"They're Mennonite dumplings," he answered.

My mom told me he was born in Russia to a Mennonite family. Stalin was waging a war on their people. I don't know what happened to his birth parents, but he was adopted, and his new mother and father brought him to B.C.

"You're gonna find us some berries?" Grandpa Merle called to my mother.

"And champagne," she said from the next room.

My grandfather mixed flour, a bit of salt, baking soda, and water in my mom's ceramic bowl. Then he pried open an eggshell. He put my mother's whisk in my hand. I stirred but couldn't get it to come together, so he took the tool and ran it through the mixture.

I studied the fourth finger on his left hand, cut off at the last knuckle. The tip of his hacked-off digit was round and smooth. If there'd been a scar, it was invisible to me. I pictured him leaning over an engine, his hand getting caught in the fan belt. As I contemplated the accident, my gut felt like I was standing at the end of the diving board at the Lowertown pool.

Grandpa Merle picked up the dough, dropped it on a cutting board, and pressed his hands into it. He sliced the dough into strips, then gumball sized clumps.

My mom came back and pulled a bag of blueberries from the freezer and placed it on the counter. My grandfather opened the bag and spooned berries into the dough balls, shaping them into pockets. He cupped my hand to show me. His skin was coarse and covered with flour, and my neck muscles stiffened.

My grandpa put the verenekies in boiling water. Soon they floated and he scooped them out with my mom's slotted spoon. He gazed out the kitchen window at our little backyard and said, "I'll come back in the summer and build you a treehouse."

There weren't any trees that were big enough, so I pictured a wooden structure on stilts. If my mother went back to the psych ward and my dad worked all the time, I'd have a place of my own.

The three of us sat down to eat. Stacked and cooling in my mom's Pyrex serving dish with pink flowers on its side, the verenekies looked like oversized slugs. They were bland. All that build-up and for what?

My grandfather made smacking sounds as he chewed. His lips were blue from the berries and his false teeth dislodged in his mouth. He fudged around with his tongue to get them back on his gums.

"The recipe calls for baking powder," he said. "But you put out baking soda."

My mom rolled her eyes and took her plate to the kitchen. Grandpa Merle trudged up the stairs and I heard him stretch out on the mattress.

I looked through the kitchen window. The yard was covered with snow. Someone's dog had left fresh turds. As my mother rinsed the dishes, I told her my grandfather said he'd come back and build a treehouse.

My mom set the dish scrubber in the sink.

"I've waited forever for him," she said. "Don't make that mistake."

***

My dad had the next day off. The smell of his coffee in the morning rose up the stairs. He listened to radio news. A reporter on a crackly line was talking about the famine in Ethiopia.

I pretended to sleep. My grandpa cleared his throat, got up, and walked downstairs. He told my father he needed to take the station wagon.

"Nothing's open," my dad said.

"I won't be long."

My father handed my grandpa his keys. My grandfather opened and clanged the car door shut, started it, and drove down the street.

When he came back an hour or so later, he told us to come outside. My dad walked out behind my grandpa, and my mom and I followed. My grandfather lifted the trunk door. Inside was a used Yamaha motorbike that he found in the classifieds. It had tall tires, a long black seat, and a dark green gas tank. Grandpa Merle lifted it out, placed it upright, and brought its kickstand down with his boot. My mother gave him a look and my dad's jaw clenched.

My grandfather took a white helmet with a blue racing stripe from the trunk, pushed it onto my head, and buckled the chin strap.

"Ask your friends to tell their parents to get them motorbikes too," he said. "You can make a gang and call yourselves the Red Devils." I nodded, but if he knew me, he wouldn't have bought me a motorcycle. I'd have asked for a Walkman, Converse high-tops, or a salamander tank.

Later, my dad drove my grandfather and me to the edge of the city. He parked outside a warehouse that had been converted into an indoor motocross track. Grandpa Merle pushed the bike inside.

The building was massive. A dirt track wove around the edge of the place. A couple of riders whipped past us.

My grandfather straddled the bike and kicked the starter. He turned the handlebar and fired up the engine. Then he motioned for me to get on. My grandpa scooted back, and I sat with his arms around me.

He put the Yamaha in gear and released the clutch. As we gained momentum, he shoved my back and hopped off. The bike wobbled and I kept my eyes on the track.

The first couple of loops, I didn't go that fast. When I passed my grandfather and dad, they were in each other's faces and ignored me. Each time I finished a lap, I observed their mouths moving but couldn't make out their words through the helmet.

I made three or four loops, pushing myself to go quicker. From the far side of the track, I saw them leave the building. That's when I lost control of the motorbike and wound up under it, the gas tank pressing against my thigh.

It took a moment to feel a burning sensation. I didn't push the bike off, because I kind of liked how it hurt, and I lay there a bit longer.

That night, Grandpa Merle left my room and went downstairs. He put on his coat and boots. As he shut the door, the house shook. My room felt empty without him, and his smell lingered.

Someone showed up at the front door. My mom came out of her room and opened it.

"Your father?" a woman's voice said.

"I'm sorry," my mother replied. "I'm so sorry."

"Found him in my garage," the woman said. "Pants at his ankles."

My mother exhaled and the neighbour left. My grandfather took off his boots.

"I think you're confused," my mom said.

"Who's the mental case?" he replied.

"There must be a bus tomorrow."

"You're pushing me out."

"You've been here for days."

In the morning, my grandpa hauled his bag from my room. Before he left, he pulled me to him and tousled my head with his hand and finger lobbed off at the knuckle.

"Whatever your mother tells you, don't forget that I tried," he said.

My mom rolled up the foamie in my room and I went to the kitchen. I opened the fridge and took out the Pyrex dish with the leftover verenekies. I thought about eating them to fill the void, but I remembered they were tasteless and chalky.

Then I did what no one had done. I took the bin from under the sink and tipped in the dumplings.

The Easter Dress

Dawn Major

Her bed trembled, her apartment trembled, her whole body trembled and in her nightmare the brakes from the train screeched—metal on metal like an echo of an old scream. Amid waking and sleep, the engineer blew his horn and light exploded through the sliding glass doors of her balcony. From the gaps between the train's freight cars flashing red and blue lights bled over from the house on the other side of the tracks. A show of Shadow Fighters played on her bedroom wall; it was a dangerous dance—a figure of a man, a figure of a woman, a boy, a jumping dog, and sirens, the soundtrack. And as quick as it had begun, the dance was over. The train came to a halt. With the ceasefire, the woman jolted awake.

Marietta, GA: In the morning, a CSX train trundled towards her apartment building hauling what not and heading wherever—Atlanta, Montgomery, Mobile—and from where she sat on an aluminum lawn chair on her second story balcony, she watched. Between her apartment building and parking lot there was a retaining wall and a graveled sloping hill covered with white boulders leading up to the train tracks. Her view sat in direct line with the tracks and maybe fifty yards from her building in Marietta Square there was a train crossing; the train stopped night and day. She hadn't considered the train when she moved into the apartment and how it would become a constant in her life as much In the morning, they rode the monorail into the park and when they asked for over-priced, chocolate-dipped, frozen bananas they got them. At the "Pirates of the Caribbean" she boarded the boats with her sisters and mother and they floated leisurely through the bayou. The Spanish moss on the Cypress trees hung like curtains over the marsh, fireflies popped with light, and crickets chirped to the soft plucking of "Oh! Susanna" playing in the background. Before entering the dark cave, before the boat plunged down a waterfall, a talking skull warned: "Dead men tell no tales!" It went dark, chilly air wafted over the back of her neck slightly blowing her hair up, and cold water splashed onto her petite arms. Even as she sailed towards danger it was better, better than remembering what made her cry the night before. And because nothing during these days at Disneyland was denied no matter the price, she lived in an unending state of magical terrorism.

The room had started to vibrate. Her parents were in one of their standoffs that reminded her of the Westerns she used to watch with her father. But it was her dance move now. So, she switched from the Fischer Price castle to her Barbie mansion and said, "Look at Barbie. She's going up the elevator. Watch. *Watch.* You aren't watching. Mommy, Daddy, watch—"

Her mother held her palm out and said, "Not now, Dandy. I'm talking to your father."

Since Barbie hadn't worked, she got up and started to do jumping-jacks. One jumping jack, two jumping jacks, three jumping jacks. While she turned her arms and legs into "X's" and I's," she recited, *Jack and Jill went up the hill to fetch a pale of water. Jack fell down and broke his crown and Jill came tumbling after.*

For a second, she thought she had gotten her father's attention. But he was just gazing back at her through blurry eyes like he was peering at something very far away.

Her mother finally relented and returned Tom Jones to his spot in the record tower.

"Fine. I'll do it. On *Easter*, even on *Easter*," the girl's mother growled, "On Easter, Peter. And, Dandy…" She growled at her in the same tone she used for her father, "you need to clean up your mess. Dinner's in ten minutes."

"……" thump, thump, thump.

When she heard the screen door slam again, she started loading her Weeble Wobbles into their treehouse. She pinched herself when she pushed the treetop down. Dammit, she used to pinch herself on that stupid tree house all the time. It hurt, but the pain was familiar having done it a thousand times. Still, it had made her want to cry. She swallowed it back.

Fifteen minutes later her mother called, "Dinnnnnnerrrr! Come on girls." She didn't bother to call for her father. He wasn't going to budge from his spot. Until later.

After dinner Amy helped her mother clean up. When Amy picked up her father's plate. her mother shook her head "no" and said, "Leave it," and Amy put it back down and wiped around the plate.

To Jackie her mother said, "Get the newspapers and spread them out."

Old papers sat on the seat of what her mother used to refer to as a gossip chair.

When everything was set, her mother filled a pot with water and put it on the burner to boil. From the cabinets she took out vinegar and food coloring.

Relief washed over the girl and her sisters, but they didn't sigh, not a peep, because anything might jinx this fragile moment and they wouldn't get to dye Easter eggs like they were promised.

Earlier in the day her mother had boiled the eggs and put them in the refrigerator. When no one was around, the girl and Jackie snuck into the kitchen and pulled the cartons out. They held their cold delicate bodies in their hands and like they had with the colors of their Easter dresses, decided which eggs would be green, which eggs would be blue and which eggs would be lavender.

Her mother placed two cartons of eggs on the table lining them up like troops next to four cereal bowls containing blue, green, red, and yellow dye. Her sisters were already well-practiced at dying Easter eggs so her mother showed her how to dip the eggs into the different colors.

"I want to make it lavender to match my dress," she said and her mother gave her a brief smile.

Amy was silent delicately dipping her eggs and Jackie had begun to sing, "Here Comes the Sun."

When she noticed the tops of her fingers had turned blue she said, "Look, Mommy," but her mother only hmm-hmmed her, because her mother was solely focused on two things: her father's hamburger and their orange and avocado green wall clock. There was a secret alarm about to go off inside her mother. She'd seen it throughout the years. Her mother looked at the clock, then looked at the hamburger. The clock, the hamburger, the clock-hamburger, clockhamburger, clockhamburger, CLOCKHAMBURGER.

In her teens, when she replayed the scenes from that night in her head, she often blamed the Easter holiday and all the pomp and circumstance around their Easter dresses and getting everything just so. Sometimes, she thought it was her mother's fault, her father's fault, even the clockhamburger's fault.

From the living room, the girl heard her father snoring and she hoped that this would be it for him for the night. In the morning when she got up to pee she sometimes found him on the bathroom floor. He was over six feet tall, but managed to look like a baby curled around the toilet on the aquamarine colored tile. She used to put her bare feet on his shoulders and squeeze the skin on his back with her toes. And if he looked cold, she put her blanky—the one she had since she was a baby—over him before going back to bed.

When the snoring got louder, her mother paused in the middle of dipping an egg into red dye then dropped its half pink, half white body back in the egg carton and sprung from her chair as if she heard someone knocking on the door. She called behind her, "Want to hear Copa girls?"

There was no reason to ask. She knew the answer, because they loved Barry Manilow.

She still remembered the feeling she had that night. She clearly recalled the anticipation of Copa Cabana coming on, first a silence, then the scratchy sound of the needle making contact with the vinyl, then pure volume.

Her name was Lola, she was a showgirl. With yellow feathers in her hair and a dress cut down to there. She would merengue, and do the cha-cha. And while she tried to be a star, Tony always tended bar.

Her mother returned, sat back in her chair, and plucked up the egg she had just abused. Pink dye had trickled over the white half of the egg. It looked like the blood that dripped down a horror movie poster. Her mother wore a determined smile while she soundlessly dipped her egg back into the red dye.

...His name was Rico. He wore a diamond. He was escorted to his chair, he saw Lola dancing there. And when she finished, he called her over. But Rico went a bit too far, Tony sailed across the bar.

There was loud scratch. The music, over.

With his bongos lying sideways on his hip, her father lurched zombielike into the kitchen and sort of fell-sat in his chair. The wood on his bongos clinked against the metal edge of his seat.

Slaw juice had leaked through his paper plate. The baked beans were dried out. Her father reached for the ketchup, but before he could lift his bun from the hamburger patty, her mother flew from her chair across the table, snatched up his burger, and smashed it into his face.

She giggled. It was funny seeing her mother smash a hamburger into her father's face. And for just a second, she forgot who he was and that this wasn't a big funny joke. Her mother laughed too. Her laugh was more mocking laugh, gleeful at delivering retribution for him ruining Easter weekend. A gotcha, sucker laugh.

With bits of cheese and ground beef still clinging to his goatee, her father rose up like a bear on its hind legs, knocked his chair into the wall behind him and leapt at her mother who had started to run towards the screen door. He managed to catch hold of her mother's terrycloth tank top and then her shoulder and he pulled her back so that she was facing him. He forcefully swung his fist into her lips. The whole time his bongos swung from side to side.

Bowls of red and blue dye toppled across the table like a river; when the colors met they turned purple, not quite lavender, but close. The dye streamed over the edge of the table onto the girl and she didn't know if she should try to clean up the mess or hide from the raging battle. She slid out of her chair and crawled under the table to hide while Easter eggs rained down from the table shattering on the floor. Their cracked shells—like puzzle pieces.

She heard Jackie cry out, "Stop, stop! Just wait," but no one was listening.

She saw Amy's legs and she knew she was making a dash for the phone, but her father must have realized this too, because she then saw Amy's legs lift off the floor as she flew into the gossip chair.

She edged closer to check on her sisters and her mother who were frozen in place watching her father as he went for the phone. With both hands he yanked, yanked, yanked until he'd freed the phone from the wall. Then he pulled his shoulder back, much like Tom Jones with his microphone, and pitched the phone into the screen door. The top hinges gave out. The door fell to the side leaving an opening at the bottom for the girl's Lhasa Apso, Raffles, who loved her mother, to run inside. Raffles stood between her father and mother snarling at her father and defending her mother who was now kneeling on the linoleum floor. That dog never had any sense of self-preservation when it came to her mother.

Her father backed away from Raffles and her mother. He scanned the scene he'd created as though lost or as if he'd forgotten what had just happened. He sunk into his chair and blindly reached for his fork, but his plate was long gone face down on the floor. The chip bowl that was still in the middle of the table had survived, however. He grabbed a handful and shoved the chips in his mouth. He hadn't eaten in over a week.

"Go to Maggie's! Go!" Her mother screamed, spitting blood from her mouth while she rose from the floor. She moved like a woman who had aged 100 years in the span of the fight. She walked towards the sink, turned on the faucet, and hung her head under the running tap water. She filled her hand with water, slurped, and spit. Bloody saliva as pink as one of the lost Easter eggs oozed into the sink. Her mother had started to moan.

With her mother moaning in the sink, the horror finally set in and the girl and Jackie, who had climbed under the table with her after the phone incident, started sobbing. Only Amy was mute as she cautiously walked past their father towards escape.

From the sink, her mother turned around and yelled, "Go! Go to Maggie's!" and that's when she noticed her mother's torn lip and where her mother's front tooth once was—a gaping hole. Blood flowed down her chin onto her neck and her terrycloth tank top with one strap torn and dangling.

Realizing that her daughters hadn't left and that they were glued to the spot shaking and sobbing, her mother screamed again, "Go! Go to Maggie's!" But how could they leave their mother with the monster her father had turned into?

As her daughters remained frozen with fear, something shifted in her mother. She stopped moaning. Fear was replaced by rage and the rage came off her mother's body like heatwaves on hot asphalt. She called him one mean name after the other. She was so full of names and mean things that in an effort to shut her up, her father rose and in one stride and forcefully grabbed the hair on the back of her mother's head and started banging her mother's head into the sink basin. Raffles barked and nipped at her father's ankles but he easily kicked him away, and the dog giving up, scampered outside.

With her father doing his damage at the sink, Amy pulled the girl and Jackie out from under the table and this time they did run.

Amy held the doorbell down while the girl and Jackie banged on the front door.

"What's happening? What's going on?" She heard from behind the door. The porch light switched on and Maggie, their next door neighbor, opened her front door.

Maggie said, "Oh, my God! What happened?" But this wasn't the first time the girl and her sisters had shown up on Maggie's doorstep; she scooped them up.

One of Maggie's boyfriends was visiting and when he saw the girl and her sisters he asked just like Maggie, "what happened?" and then "Is your mother still there?"

Three little sobbing voices told the same now familiar story. Slamming, pushing, clawing, tearing, pounding. Blood, teeth, hair, bones.

Maggie's boyfriend went towards the front door, but Maggie told him "no" while she herded the girl and her sisters into the bedroom and told them to all hide in the closet.

Through the open louver doors, she watched Maggie, who was dressed in one of those sexy long dresses her mother took to go see Tom Jones, standing over the nightstand yelling demands into the phone at who she later realized was the Los Angeles police department.

"When? How long?" Maggie's voice sounded panicked. She dropped the receiver onto the cradle, dashed to her window, pulled the drapes aside, and peeped through the blinds, repeating, "Come on, Come on."

Maggie's boyfriend stood next to Maggie, his arms stiffly at his side with his hands made into fists. He kept saying, "Let me go over there," and "I'll take care of him," but she heard Maggie hiss, "He's got a gun and he's used it before. You're staying. I got this."

Maggie was the opposite of her mother. She had older kids who didn't live with her and she had lots of boyfriends. There was always a stream of Cadillacs and Continentals parked in her driveway. Their elongated opulent bodies stretched out unapologetic, ready. Her father used to refer to Maggie as the LA Magdalene; the girl never got the reference until she was in her teens.

The girl was never allowed in Maggie's bedroom, but sometimes she said she needed to pee and rather than going to the bathroom she sneaked in Maggie's room. Everything in Maggie's bedroom was red, white, and gold. The carpeting was a reg shag. A heavy red and gold, velvet, brocade quilt covered her bed which was surrounded by layers of sheer red curtains that hung from the ceiling. The window treatments were made out of the same material as the quilt, and on either side of Maggie's bed were white and gold, faux marble nightstands suspended from the ceiling by thick gold chains. On both nightstands there were always heavy crystal ashtrays full of cigarette butts. Maggie's room was a throne room for a queen, but looking back, it was more like a tawdry boudoir.

The girl crept into Maggie's closet, closed her eyes tight and made herself go very small. And even though one of Maggie's high heels dug into her leg; she ignored it, becoming smaller and smaller, as small as one of her Fisher Price Play Family people. Not invisible, but small enough that if anyone looked inside Maggie's closet, they'd miss her.

When the police didn't show, Maggie called again. At one point Maggie broke a nail from frantically dialing the rotary. She breathed, fuck, and sucked her finger. Maggie kept calling, then walking to the window, then calling, and then pacing back and forth. It was a lot like the back and forth that her mother and father did that afternoon.

Once, while Maggie's boyfriend worked the phone, Maggie came over and sat on the floor outside the closet doors and talked to the girl and her sisters as though they were puppies, "How are my three little pigs? Don't cry. Shh..shh…don't cry. Please stop crying. Which little pig gets the brick house, the stick house, the straw?" But they were way past playing games and had retreated into their safehouses.

Amy started counting the number of times Maggie or Maggie's boyfriend called. One of her hands was a closed fist, the other fingers fixed at five. Jackie hummed, *Who shot who? Who shot who?* While sucking her thumb and rocking back and forth as if she was sitting on a rocking chair.

To stop crying, the girl became a speck, a speck deep in the haunted caves of Dead Man's Grotto, back in *her* safehouse at Disneyland. She had run away with Tom Sawyer and Huck Finn to become pirates. Tom and Huck chased her over the bridge to Smuggler's Cove.

When Maggie called a sixth time, Amy's index finger shot out as fast as a gunslinger and the girl was back to her normal size. She was back in Maggie's closet and she knew deep down they weren't going to wear their Easter dresses, their gloves, their patent leather Mary Janes. There would be no dainty purses. The Easter eggs were ruined. There would be no Easter bunny. No Easter at all.

She tugged Amy's tee-shirt and, because they were hiding, whispered, "Will we get to wear our dresses?"

Amy shushed her, but she really wanted to know so she tugged on her tee-shirt again and asked, "Do you think the Easter Bunny will still come?"

Her sister turned her head, looked at her in a cruel way, and said, "No! We're not having Easter!" Then Amy went back to watching Maggie.

She couldn't hold back the tears anymore. She gave into sobbing, "No Easter, no, no, no Easter Bunny, *no, no, no*."

On the seventh time Maggie called, she didn't ask "when" or "how long?" She cursed those *lazy-useless-good-for-nothing* cops up and down. She was seething and spewing evil words. And when she later envisioned Maggie surrounded by all that red and gold it seemed as though Maggie's bedroom was hell, that they were in hell, and Maggie was witch, who had invoked demons—*Lucifer, Lilith, Beelzebub, Ashura, Mephistopheles, Hades, Loki*—because only then after cursing them, did the police show themselves.

That night after Maggie's boyfriend left, she slept in Maggie's fancy bed between her sisters. Blue and red lights from the police cars and the ambulance flashed through Maggie's red sheer curtains. Her mother had shown her how to turn red and blue into purple. She told her if she didn't leave her Easter egg in the purple dye too long, it would turn lavender like her dress. So, that's what she did that night before Easter Sunday. She made lavender Easter eggs out of the lights streaming through the curtains of Maggie's bed.

A month later from that horrendous night when everything was stitched up, when bruises had faded, and they were a happy family again, the girl helped mother get her into her Easter dress. Before they left for Mass, her father took a picture of their pretend Easter in their front yard and when they got home from church, huge Easter baskets were waiting. Their old Easter baskets had been replaced by huge baskets—monuments brimming with candy, bigger than any of her friend's baskets. After she hunted Easter eggs in the backyard, she sat in the dining room to eat "Easter" dinner and her father forked ham out onto her plate. Easy Peasy.

She recognized that woman and mother across the tracks with her lavender dress. She spoke her language. *Stay. Don't run away.*

Pretend. And when it all goes to shit, there's Disneyland. She'd spent a good amount of time at Disneyland when she was a child.

She knew that mother and son's story like she knew that in the morning come Easter Sunday that woman would hide Easter eggs and later her son would hunt them like he had discovered gems right there in his own backyard even if "Easter" was ten days later, a month later, he'd get his happy family and his God-dam Easter basket.

She knew that story by heart. If she could have leapt across the tracks, she'd grab up that little boy, and tell him it was all bull-shit. To hop, hop, hop away. But she did none of that; she just watched the wind whipping the woman's lavender dress dry.

Later in the afternoon, when the mother brought an ironing board out to the porch she once again imagined the sound of the screen door slamming behind the mother like she imagined the shrill sound of the ironing board's metal collapsible legs when the mother unfolded them.

She watched as the mother plugged the iron into a socket, set the iron on the ironing board, and then rose on her tippy toes to take down her lavender dress.

For a minute or two, waiting for the iron to heat, the mother regarded the empty train tracks. Maybe the mother was observing her, this woman who sat on her balcony watching trains go by, but the mother only looked over for a moment before licking her finger and lightly touching the iron.

The mother delicately placed her lavender Easter dress on the ironing board. She sprayed a light coat of starch over the dress. She picked up the iron and with the hot metal iron she pressed out its wounds, made clean lines where there were once scratches.

A breeze had picked up and for a second she stopped observing the mother in order to gaze at the sky. She breathed in minerals, or petrichor. Raindrops dusted the asphalt parking lot below her balcony. Spring rain to wash it all away. With the rainstorm, the mother stopped ironing. She folded her lavender Easter dress over one arm, then yanked the iron's cord out of the socket and ran inside with both the dress and the hot iron.

This time she swore she heard the screen door slam.

And then as quickly as the rain began, it was over. Here comes the sun. The slick bluish-black asphalt dried to gray. The rain washed yellow pollen off the white rocks from the slope below the train tracks and the red clay blushed a deep coral color.

Her own mother's bruises had faded long ago.

In the distance, she heard that familiar sound of a train approaching and she wondered how big the son's Easter basket would be. Would the little boy wear a lavender bow tie to match his mother's lavender dress? Would his father take their Easter photo and later slice the ham?

Yes, yes. All of it.

Tender

Souad Zakarani

From the window of their apartment, Will watched Juma downstairs fumble with her keys. The man beside her was looking at the dirty ground. The gate stuck. Then they were upstairs. She had not been crying, but there was the strain of cheerfulness all over her. She unbuttoned her coat.

"Will," she said, "it's Marcus. You remember Marcus."

"We've never met," said Will. He stuck out his hand. In fact, though he had seen a photograph of Marcus just a few days ago, slipped out from between the pages of Juma's journal, he still wouldn't have been able to recognize the man standing in front of him without a bit of prompting. This Marcus had a scrappy beard. There were holes in his tennis shoes, and his jeans were baggy and smeared with dirt. The smell coming off him was intensely physical, sour and frighteningly animal. Like an aura, it quivered around him, slowly expanding to fill the room.

Marcus's hand was warm and dry. But he wouldn't look up to meet Will's eyes.

"Good to meet you, man," said Will.

Juma had hung her coat up, now she was standing there in the foyer, eyeing them both. "Marcus," she said. "The bathroom's just over here. I'll get you a towel and you can have a hot shower."

Marcus nodded. While he wouldn't look at Will, he would look at her, at Juma. She tugged at her hair. Her eyes were on him.

"Are you hungry? You must be hungry," said Juma.

"I'm fine." His voice was deep and dry, somewhat distant.

"You can wash up and we'll make dinner."

He shrugged. "Don't put yourself out."

When they heard the water go on, Juma said, "I should just chuck his clothes, right?"

"What's he going to wear?"

"I thought he could borrow something of yours."

"Won't he feel offended if you throw his clothes away?"

"I guess we could just wash them. Should we just wash them?"

It was strange for Will to see Juma like this, so uncertain.

"I don't know."

"Do you have any clothes he can borrow?"

"Not really."

"Okay," she said. She put one of her shoes back on, hard and shiny, leather with a sharp heel. "I'll go and get some clothes for him."

"Go where?"

"I don't know." Her lips became full, and her eyes, a redness coming into her face. It looked like anger.

"Come here," he said.

She would not, so he went to her, and put his arms around her. She smelled clean, of lemon and vanilla, and salt. She put her fists against him, but her body softened. "I have to go get him some new clothes."

"I have clothes," he said. Holding her, he was soothed, she was his. "They'll be big on him. It's okay."

Marcus stayed in the shower a long time. He had worked the smell off him by the time he came out. As they sat at the table, Will tried not to watch Marcus eat. His actions were careful and mannered, each mouthful he brought to his chapped lips. More than anything, it was the cast of his face that dared each person to put their eyes on him. Juma carried on a long and unbending conversation with almost no help from anyone else. She talked about the cases she was working on, the books she had read, even, sometimes, about the weather. She looked from Marcus to Will to Marcus, as though seeking approval or assurance from each face, Marcus who could not give it, Will who couldn't bring himself to. Finally Marcus said, "What happened to your paintings?"

"Oh," she said. "It felt sort of weird having them around."

"So what, you got rid of them?"

"They're in my parents' garage."

"And you're done?"

"Yes," she said, color coming into her face. "I'm done."

"You see them, Will?"

But Will had arrived to Juma too late to see the paintings—all but one. It was a huge fleshy nude, intentionally grotesque, and he was glad not to have it displayed in their living room. Anyway, the paintings had become a source of pain to her, and at one point she had talked about destroying them. Instead, they sat still untouched in her parents' garage, their faces turned to the wall.

"Marcus, is the food okay?"

"Yeah, great," said Marcus.

"Will's a good cook," said Juma.

"One of us had to be."

"Yeah, Juma can't cook for shit," said Marcus.

"I'm getting better," she said.

"She isn't," said Will.

"Marcus is pretty good too," said Juma. "He knows how to roast a chicken, anyway."

"Still do," said Marcus, lifting his eyes for only a moment.

Marcus helped clean up after dinner and then shaved in the bathroom with a borrowed razor. Will was feeling aimless. The dishes were done, and drying, the leftovers put away. He would normally sit and watch TV with a beer and Juma in the living room, but with Marcus here he couldn't do that. He sat at the kitchen table instead and watched Juma plumping the pillows until Marcus came out of the bathroom. Without the beard, Marcus looked different, very clean. His cheeks were whiskey-brown and smooth. His hair too, he had trimmed, bringing it very close to his scalp. He patted his face with a towel. Will offered him a beer, he declined. He was smaller than Will, shorter than him and firmly compacted, skinny, actually. And it was true, Will had put on some weight in the last couple years. The clothes on Marcus made him look especially small.

A long silence. Then Juma came and offered him everything: coffee, tea, beer, water, juice, and more milk. Marcus shook his head. His body seemed tense in his loose clothes. Juma looked different next to Marcus, like a color that brightens when seen next to its complement. Did they want to be left alone? For a few moments, Will, stubbornly, stayed where he was. But Juma was freezing him out, refusing to fill the air with talk like she had at dinner. Will gave in and went to brush his teeth and lay in bed. He was not at all tired, though, and tried to read a book. He could hear Juma and Marcus speaking from the other room. Her voice changed as she spoke to him. It was less firm—she phrased normal sentences like questions. Marcus's voice, on the other hand, seemed sure, he spoke little, used few words, and the silence that contracted around him made him powerful. She asked him how his mother was doing, he said that she had died. He used the words passed on. There was a small, tight silence, where Will imagined Juma gathering herself. Are you doing alright, Juma asked him. Yes fine, said Marcus, with a small, dry laugh. I'm fine. Then Juma was embarrassed for her question and changed the subject, asking if he needed anything from the grocery store. Marcus said no. You are tired, said Juma, finally. Were they touching? Had she laid her hand on his? Then the chair scraped as she stood, or he did, someone went to the bathroom, someone went about turning off all the lights, the bedroom door opened and closed and Juma was pulling her nightclothes from the dresser.

"What time is it?"

"Almost nine," he said, putting down his book. He watched her as she unbuttoned her shirt, facing away from him, reaching back to unhook the beige-colored bra. The muscles of her shoulders were tense under the skin, horse's muscles, he thought. In her nightgown, and into bed, her body slid next to his, she lay face down and began to cry.

"Juma," he said.

She would not lift her face from the pillow. He reached for her, but she curled away from him, and lay on her side, near silent, smothering her busy breathing with the pillow as he sat beside her. He picked up his book but was too angry to read it. She sat up, wiped her face, and saw him, his clenched jaw.

Then she let him hold her. She seemed to fall asleep almost immediately after he turned off the light, a talent she had, while Will lay awake for several hours. A sigh from the other room, a cough, even the body turning over on the inflatable mattress pulled him awake when he found himself sliding into the black gully. His dream was so subtle he didn't realize he was dreaming, until, with an enormous breath, his body threw itself awake. His eyes felt blurry and he couldn't make out the time. But he could feel Marcus's presence very strongly in the other room. Will got out of bed. Blue light from the window: Juma looked beautiful and dead. When he could not sleep and she could, he felt shut out of her mind unfairly. Every time he saw her like this, he had to resist the urge to wake her up.

The light was on in the kitchen. Marcus was sitting at the table. He had trimmed and scrubbed his fingernails, but there was still grit in the creases where the nail met the soft pad of flesh. A metal tumbler sweating in his hands, in the warmth of the apartment, warmth that their three bodies had made.

"Can't sleep?"

"No."

"Warm enough?"

"Fine," said Marcus, looking into the cup again.

Will filled a glass of water at the sink, suddenly thirsty. He stood there at the sink and drank it quickly, tipping his head back. But he felt vulnerable with his throat exposed and he slowed down and just sipped. He filled his glass again. Water, milk, whiskey: what was in Marcus's tumbler?

"We're getting married. Next year, September."

"Juma told me."

"She's changed a lot."

"I know."

The famous Marcus. For years, Will had imagined him, and the man in front of him was not the person he had imagined. His eyes strangest of all. They were deep, reflected copper in the light, and when they looked at him, for the first time since he'd arrived, Will felt them pass over him like an X-ray, finding and recording every flaw. It was the terror of his imagination—or was it? Marcus took a long pull at the tumbler, Will, unsettled, left the room. In bed, Juma was warm. She had thrown off the comforter, sweating. She slept sometimes as if she was swimming, with her arms flung out. However, as he lay down next to her she accepted his body, almost burying herself in it, his coolness. Sleep came just before dawn.

***

Juma and Marcus had met one afternoon at the public library. She was nineteen and he was twenty-three. She sat down on the opposite end of the table from Marcus and glanced up at him from time to time, when she thought he wasn't looking. But he was looking. When he smiled at her she was ashamed of herself and looked back down at her book. She was studying for her art history final. She looked up again. He was still looking, still smiling. He got up and introduced himself. He was a junior at City College, a philosophy major. And she? She seemed like an artist, was she? There was paint in her fingernails, no lucky guess, just an observant eye, but she looked startled at him like a mind reader. Let me guess, a painter? She nodded. In those days, she was shy. Would you like to get a drink with me? She said that it was only three. Okay, a coffee? But then she changed her mind and said, no, a drink. She followed him down the steps of the library and out to the street. Feeling nineteen, wholly nineteen, impulsive, full-bodied and young. He had terrific posture and wore a white shirt with a pressed collar, looking, as he moved down the street, like a waiter or a dancer. It was dark in the bar he chose, he bought her a beer. Each time the door opened the light fell directly onto his face, curving over his clean cheeks, his wet eyes. He was from Baltimore, the first of his family to go to college, they thought he was crazy for studying philosophy. Try getting a degree in fine art, she told him. About the same, he said. Equally crazy. As soon as she had finished her beer she wanted to kiss him, but she still held herself away, not touching him, not even turning her body toward him, but pointing it straight ahead and resting her elbows on the bar. It was her face she turned slightly and her eyes. You want another? She shook her head. Four thirty, but late in winter and the sun was going down as they left. And where to now? She said she should go home and study for her art history test. He admitted he needed to write his philosophy paper. I went to the library so I would not get distracted, he said.

Me too, she said, but I always get distracted.

Always someone who wants to distract you, I bet. They were standing in front of her bus stop. When he smiled, she saw the sweet jumble of his teeth. He kissed her mouth; she felt it immediately and all over. Juma, nineteen, fully reckless: she took him home with her. He stayed four years. Some Saturday mornings, he made her eggs, and brought them to her in bed, read Kierkegaard aloud during lazy afternoons as she fell into a warm doze: his voice troubled the surface of her dreams, made them half-lucid. On their second Christmas, he brought her to Baltimore to meet his mother, Nelda. Marcus and Nelda had the same delicate bones, though Nelda's face had grown wide and soft, burying some of the beauty that had once been there. She greeted Juma with what felt to Juma like suspicion, but later she thought it might actually have been fear: Juma's fine coat, her glossy hair and her straight teeth looked expensive, a girl accustomed to comfort and fine things. But Nelda made them tea, and brought out the customary albums of Marcus's babyhood and childhood, and the awkward years of his adolescence. There was a deep and obvious pride in the way she touched Marcus's face in the pictures, even the years of slouching, frowning.

You a painter? Will you paint my house? Nelda said.

Sure, Juma said, What color?

Green and yellow, like an Easter egg.

I thought they only paint houses colors like that in New Orleans.

Those are my favorite colors. The smile she offered Juma told her that she had been teasing, and they were, suddenly, friends.

The next morning, they opened presents, and she marveled at the gentleness between Marcus and Nelda. She got him a sweater, he had gotten her a yellow teapot and a bathrobe. Nelda gave Juma a present too, three kinds of fruit-scented lotions in a plastic pack. Juma gave her chocolates. The whole event had a tender hesitancy that was almost unbearable—each person made a great performance of delight when they opened their presents. There were tears in Nelda's eyes when they said good-bye; she brushed them away, not at all ashamed.

***

Juma's fights with Marcus were fierce and unfair. There were things she said that angered him, innocent things, she thought. They were young; she felt a terror, at times, of drowning in him. Worse yet, when the fights became bitter, and Marcus began pulling into himself, retreating into silence. And she would move to the opposite direction, screaming at him, waving her hands in his face, sometimes pulling crazily at her own hair. In the dark hours of morning, out of sheer exhaustion, they apologized and slept, though neither the sleep nor the apology was ever satisfying enough. They seemed to make do.

One New Year's Eve, they fought at a party and Juma left in a huff an hour until midnight. She expected Marcus to follow her but he did not. The bus was roiling with happy drunks; just before twelve, it deposited her in her quiet neighborhood.

You have fun at the party?

Acting like he hadn't heard her but she could see his body register her voice. The smooth muscles in his back as he lifted his shirt above his head, dark skin under the white T-shirt, darker than her skin, but warm. She wanted to press her face to it.

Marcus?

He went to the bathroom. She could hear the shower running. She began to cry. When he came out, she wiped her face and said again, Marcus?

He dressed in clean clothes. His graceful body tired. Still moving like he hadn't heard her, didn't see her in the room. If Marcus had turned to her, if he had said one thing—not even an apology—she would have asked him to stay. And he would have stayed. He knew this. He kept quiet. She bit her lips and watched him calmly pack up his belongings into suitcases and garbage bags, leaving nothing behind to pick up later.

She moved across town, shut her paintings up in her parents' garage, and turned, to their relief, to law. She was unhappy for a time, and then she was busy, and forgot to be. One day she walked out into the cold morning of winter, and felt, with surprise, the sun falling warm on her face, the clear blue of the sky.

***

In the morning, Juma had made coffee by the time Will woke, had already scrubbed out the shower from the night's grime, and was dressed for work. He found her paused in the doorway of the living room, where Marcus slept. His deep breaths whistled out of him. Morning and his skin had a kind of flatness to it, and his hair. Even in sleep, his face looked weary. Juma started.

"How long have you been standing there?" she asked.

"I just woke up."

They went to the kitchen. He needed coffee, lots of it, and poured himself a generous amount.

"Didn't sleep too well, huh?"

"No," he said. The coffee was not hot, only a little warm. "Do you know how long he's staying?"

"We haven't talked about it yet."

"You didn't think this through."

"I didn't."

Her face looked wretched, and despite the apparent ease of her slumber, unslept.

"You love him," he said.

She laid her head against his palm, open on the table. "Not like that."

Her cheek was hot. Will said, almost cruelly, "You should be somebody's mother."

When Will got home, though the apartment was empty, he began to feel as though Marcus was still in the room. He could see Marcus sitting beside him on the couch, looking down at his clasped hands, sitting in formidable silence. Was he gone for good? It seemed like it, yet the thought did not bring Will relief. He had another beer. When Juma came home, a little later than usual, she was loaded down with things. Clothes for Marcus, and shoes that fit, socks, bars of soap, a warm hat, new toothbrush, deodorant and toothpaste. She was alone and rumpled. She kissed Will at the door.

"I was worried."

"I called you. I left a message."

His phone confirmed this. "I don't know how I missed it."

"Where's Marcus?"

"I thought he might be with you."

"He didn't come back here?"

"Not that I can see."

She was putting her coat back on.

"What are you doing?"

"I have to go look for him."

"What are you going to do if you find him? Drag him bodily back to the apartment?"

"He needs help, Will."

"Sweetheart, what can we possibly do for him?" He followed her out the door, pulling on a jacket. Dark had fallen, the streetlights blinked on. Juma walked furiously down the street, looking into the faces of all the people she passed. Will stayed a few paces behind, just watching her.

Juma had loosed herself from the crowd she was crossing and began to move very quickly down the street. She turned the corner and began to climb a hill so steep there were stairs etched into the sidewalk. Will followed her. Her quick pace was sagging.

"Hey," he said.

"Hey."

"You okay?"

"I don't know," she said. She put a hand to her forehead. "I feel like I'm dreaming. Are you?"

"Yeah," he said.

"What are we going to do with all that stuff I bought?"

"Give it to Glide." Then he said, "Juma, do you remember me?"

"What do you mean?" Her eyes were fixed on him. They were sad, dark. When he looked at her, he was used to seeing himself reflected in her face, and now, he looked and looked for that sign of himself. Perhaps he'd been imagining it all along. She kissed his hand, her soft lips. Was it enough? "Of course I do."

***

She saw him. She didn't speak. She just stood there. Soon he felt her eyes on him and looked up, and an eerie feeling went through him... Juma: the force of the word through his lips had heft, velocity. In her face, he could see how low he had become. Biting her lips red.

"Marcus," she said. Suddenly it felt precious, his name. He didn't want it in her mouth.

He let her take him home, like he had all those years ago, coming to it, this time, unwilling, dazed. Language returned to him slowly—he spoke very little in his new life. But by dinner he wanted to ask if she was enjoying it. It would be to wound her: her distress was plain. Her well-intentioned distress, that some part of the world had slipped out of order, and it was her task to tuck it back into place. Groom him and feed him and let him sleep—and then? Let him go on his merry way, so she could return to the task of planning and managing current and future happiness, her trips, her wedding, her dinner parties. How different she was from the girl he had loved. It's not like he didn't remember her pettiness, her unthinking comments. And yet, he could see her through the thick screen of memory, twenty-two, full of uncertainty, drunk, dancing shyly at a party to the Talking Heads. Glancing back at him with a smile, wearing that short green dress, looking self-conscious, tugging at the hem, but dancing, with her firm legs, her long soft arms, asking with her eyes, like a child asks her parent, do you see me? Do you see me? And his eyes had said yes, I see you.

***

When he woke in their apartment in the morning, she was standing in the doorway. She whispered, "Are you awake? Marcus?"

He closed his eyes, moving away from her, falling into a thin sleep. It was warm. He had a good dream, his mother was there. He couldn't see her face but it was good to be close to her. When he woke the second time, the apartment was empty, and it was time to leave. And go—where? They had taken his clothes to wash, but he found them in a garbage bag in the hall closet and put them on, dirty.

Then he walked away.

7 Days Into the Week of a Childless Woman

Zoé Mahfouz

DAY 1

I wake up around 11 a.m. and decide to go out for brunch. On the way home, I impulsively book a spin class, followed by a weightlifting session, followed by a trampoline class because my pelvic floor is still intact. Feeling motivated, I confidently head to the gym. After my workout, I grab a protein smoothie from my favorite smoothie shop and chat with the owner, John, a Colombian man who insists on giving me his unsold goods as a token of appreciation. I graciously accept and pretend to eat them because I'm a good person who understands the rules of social interaction.

While we're chatting, I witness a child throwing a tantrum after spilling juice all over her dress. Her mother frantically searches for napkins, only for the child to grab what's left of the juice and hurl it directly into her mother's face. I go home, put on *The Mindy Project*, and watch two episodes. Then I take a nap.

DAY 2

The weather is amazing, so I take the bus to the park. I end up walking through three different parks over the span of two to three hours, petting random poodles and feeding a mix of blueberries, raspberries, and strawberries to squirrels that take them straight from my hand, making me feel like Snow White.

In the distance, I spot a child deliberately kicking one of the squirrels while her mother tries to stop her but can't keep up. She then gets into a heated argument with her husband about whose responsibility this is, but he's too busy ogling a 20-year-old jogger to care.

On my way back, I notice a showing of *Wicked* at a nearby movie theater. Even though I've already seen it twice, I decide to go for a third round. All that walking and watching has exhausted me, so when I get home, I take a nap.

DAY 3

I wake up with my Korean face mask still on and gently peel it off, admiring my glass-skin effect. My hair, soaked in overnight oil and wrapped in a towel, gets a thorough wash because today I have a photoshoot. I savor the solitude of my bathroom, enjoying the silence.

I pack my small suitcase and head to the shoot, where my hair and makeup are done professionally. I post a few TikToks for fun and end up having a fantastic photoshoot that lasts longer than expected. The photographer casually tells me I have a great body, unlike his wife, "whose body has been ruined by two pregnancies." He then confides in me that they've decided to become polyamorous.

On my way back, I stop at the grocery store and have a quick chat with the security guard. Meanwhile, a child launches himself into a man's shopping cart, causing it to topple over and send cucumbers, tomatoes, and celery rolling everywhere. The kid bursts into hysterical tears as his mother gets bombarded with judgmental stares and disapproving nods from surrounding shoppers.

When I get home, I start a load of laundry and hear on the radio news that a woman has been arrested for putting her two-year-old in a washing machine. I then have an uninterrupted, hour-and-a-half-long phone call with my mom. After that, I take a nap.

DAY 4

It's raining, so I decide to spend the afternoon at a museum. I grab a protein bar and head out around lunchtime.

At the ticket counter, I notice a group of children wailing because their mother wants to take them to the museum restaurant instead of McDonald's. They retaliate by attempting to destroy a 100-year-old statue, which results in them being thrown out by security guards who immediately regret touching them upon realizing their hands are now inexplicably sticky.

I take an audio guide and stroll leisurely through the exhibit, taking my time in front of each painting. Feeling sufficiently cultured, I stop by a local pizzeria I often order from on UberEats and finally try their pizza in person. I savor a giant pepperoni pizza with a side of garlic dip because I'm not planning on kissing anyone today.

A family walks in with strollers and crying babies, prompting a waiter to rush over and inform them that they don't have a kids' menu or highchairs. Chaos ensues as the children start rolling on the floor, shrieking, "I'm hungry! I'm hungry!" while the rest of the restaurant shoots the mother dirty looks.

Satisfied with my day, I go home and take a nap.

DAY 5

Before leaving for my screenwriting class, I mop my apartment floors and leave the windows open to dry them. I feel comfortable leaving my home unattended because I know everything will still be exactly as I left it when I return.

Since I arrive at class early, I stop by the protein shop to stock up on coconut bars and chat with my favorite employee, Dayo, who looks like death warmed over. He tells me his toddler is teething and hasn't slept in days.

When I finally get to class, the secretary informs us that the lesson will be conducted online because the instructor couldn't find daycare due to a strike and is now quarantined at home with her kids, who have lice. I endure the awkward virtual class, then go home and take a nap.

DAY 6

I have a long weekend ahead, so I decide to book a trip to Italy with my mom. We're thrilled to find a hotel with a pool until we read TripAdvisor reviews warning that it's frequently closed because parents keep bringing their diapered children in, and, well... let's just say the water gets contaminated beyond repair.

We wisely opt for an adults-only hotel instead.

To celebrate, we put on some music to get into vacation mode. Moments later, there's furious banging on the front door. It's our downstairs neighbor, barefoot and enraged, ranting that our music woke up his toddler and now their afternoon is ruined. Too bad, because now I feel exhausted and am about to take a well-deserved nap.

DAY 7

I take my spotless car out for a drive, rent an entire bouncy castle just for myself, strip naked, and gleefully jump around while watching the live Academy Awards ceremony on my phone and devouring ice cream in every flavor imaginable, because I can.

Then, I call my GP to inquire about the procedure for getting my uterus removed. This conversation fills me with an unexpected surge of excitement.

It's been an emotional rollercoaster of a day, so I take a nap.

I Am The Animal

Don Edwards

I am the animal that knows that it knows
Closer still to grizzly than to Jesus,
The barrel chested creature
Strewing slobber and poetry throughout its den —
Tripping over the broken skulls of symbols,
Gnawing on the discarded femurs of cadence and rhyme.

I can think a bridge or posit a concept.
I can build a portfolio and retire to the islands.
I can kick you across the face and break your jaw.
I can steal your wife and make her forget who you are.
I can make children like any monkey
And claim them to be uniquely soulful.
But that won't be enough —
Give me the ring for catharsis
So I can stay between the lines.
There I'll lose the itch that followed me in.
Crawl on after if you wish
And take that if you dare to
And that and that as well.
Help make my knotted disposition unwind.

Yes I am the animal still acknowledging consequence
But often lacking regard,

The one who follows gods and women,
While sniffing the air for my next kill,
Then kneeling before a pool of water and stone altars
To get me through another day.

See me for what I am — reaching for heaven
While eating the dirt of the world I inhabit
And applying a healing violence
To calm my furry soul.

The Classic Escape

Micah Ward

The sun doesn't rise dramatically over the landscape of smoke stacks and bare limbed trees. The day simply becomes lighter, as if a bulb is gradually intensifying its light. Rhonda emerges from the back seat of the car onto the sidewalk in front of her house. Smoke wafts from the exhaust. Giggles and laughs follow her as she waves and weaves her way to the porch and front door.

In the kitchen her mother scrambles eggs and eyes Rhonda with disgust.

"Your shift starts in an hour and I can smell the liquor on you all the way over here. Why?"

"Why what?"

"Why aren't you getting serious with your life? Ever since the divorce and moving back in with your father and me, all you do is go out with those hoodlum girlfriends of yours and drink all night. Is that why Tony left you? Is this what you did when you were married to him?"

Rhonda pours a cup of coffee, "Leave Tony out of this. I'm just trying to have a little fun for a change."

"Your little fun will get you fired. Go wash that stink off before you go to work."

Rhonda labors up the staircase feeling the impending hangover that she will take with her to the mill and her work station where she will watch the clock tick toward morning break. Then lunch. Then afternoon break and gloriously, quitting time. Another changeless day leading to a silent and reproachful dinner with her parents.

At the end of this day, she returns to her childhood bedroom and naps until her phone rings.

"Oh, hell yeah, I'll be ready in half an hour."

Rhonda is on her feet and heading to the bathroom to freshen up. She trots down the stairs and sees the waiting car at the sidewalk and hears her mother's, "Oh, for the love of God Rhonda, not again tonight!"

"I'll be early, don't wait up," and Rhonda is gone.

Her father doesn't turn his attention from the television.

The girls giggle and pass a bottle of bottom shelf scotch around the car. Six of them packed into a clunker that is older than any one of its occupants. A fog of cigarette smoke leaks from the windows of the car as they pull into the parking lot of their favorite dive.

Dodging mud and sliding on patches of ice they laugh their way across the lot and into the tavern. Smoke pools near the ceiling and billiard balls clack loud enough to be heard over the blare of the jukebox. Greetings are shouted and returned in every direction.

One of Rhonda's friends nudges her with her elbow and says, "Look who's over there."

Rhonda looks and sees Tony. He sees her. They manage to simultaneously ignore and sneak glances at each other for the next hour. The inevitable must happen. It always does for those whose poor choices begat even poorer ones. Rhonda borrows the car keys and follows Tony outside. There is no conversation. The windows steam into gray curtains. The ancient shocks of the car squeak as it rocks back and forth.

Afterwards, they fumble to close zippers and button various pieces of clothing and Tony asks, "Are you still working at the mill?"

"What else am I going to do around here? Join the country club?"

They climb out of the car and light cigarettes in the cold Minnesota night. Tony leans against the fender and says, "I'm getting out of here Rhonda."

"Where are you going?"

"I've joined the Army. I leave for boot camp next Tuesday."

The two stand there in silence shivering slightly as the wind increases.

"The Army," she says.

"Yeah," he replies. "I've been out of work for most of the last three months and they said I could learn how to operate heavy equipment in the engineers. Hey, at least I get out of this mill town and see some of the rest of the world."

Rhonda shakes her head and ponders the classic escape from small-town frustration. Join the Army.

Two months later she sits at the breakfast table with her parents before they all leave for work.

"This is a pleasant change," her mother says. "Like the old days when you weren't hung over every morning and we had nice meals together."

Rhonda looks at her mother and says, "Yeah, mom, some things have to change sooner or later. I've had my fun running with the girls. I've got to do something better than just living here and working in that mill for the rest of my life."

Her father looks up with a curious expression.

Rhonda drops the bombshell, "I'm joining the Army."

When the stunned silence has stretched long enough Rhonda continues, "The recruiter told me that my test scores qualify for medic training. When I get out the GI Bill will pay for college. I could be a nurse someday. Army pay's not great but it beats the mill and maybe I'll get to see some of the world."

Silence descends again until Rhonda's mother looks at her husband and speaks. "Ralph, say something."

Ralph glances at his wife then looks Rhonda directly in the eyes. "I believe that's the smartest damn thing you've said since high school. Good luck."

Rhonda smiles at her old man and then kisses his bald head as she leaves the kitchen. She pulls her coat snug against the winter chill. She thinks that she would like to be stationed in a warm climate. Anything to get out of the northern Minnesota winters.

She thinks about being a nurse someday and her eyes fill with tears as she thinks about a decision she must make. She thinks about the bathroom before she left the house and the test strip that read positive.

Buried Treasure

Celia Miles

We sisters were fools for burying our treasures—and for digging them up. In the sunlight we pulled the battered shoebox from the shallow hole where we'd placed it two days earlier. All there—only slightly grimy: three buckeyes, a blue bottle with water diluting the smell of Evening in Paris, my lucky, run-over-by-a-train penny. Satisfied, my sisters and I tucked our treasures in our pockets and headed toward home.

We lived near the Jaspers. Mr. and Mrs. Jasper boarded three city men, men who were scouting for stands of curly walnut. They had a lot of money, wallets bulging with it. So they enjoyed flipping pennies to us if we drifted over to the fringes of the Jasper yard in the last glimmer of sunlight. They'd been well fed and sat in rocking chairs on the front porch with their feet stretched out in front of them. Their cigars were a wonder to us. We knew not to bother the paying guests, not to get too close. When they caught sight of us, the men dug into their pockets for loose change. They grinned when we scrambled for the coins. I heard one of them mutter, "Like little chickens, aren't they?"

Anyway, we kept our pennies and nickels in small, red-checked bags with drawstrings that Mrs. Jasper had made out of cloth scraps. After we picked up pennies and even a silver dime that evening, Georgie, a neighbor boy, intercepted us. He gathered us around to tell us about his adventure at the traveling carnival. "I heard the dangest story from the world's oldest man," he said. His voice cracked just a little; at thirteen we never knew exactly how he'd sound.

"What? Tell us." My sisters were big-eyed. Georgie didn't pay much attention to them usually. I hung back, not exactly trusting him and his practical jokes.

"Well, this man—older than Jericho, I reckon—this man said he knew for a fact that if you planted money just at the right time of the year and the right time of the moon, it'd grow! That's what he said."

"And you believe that?" I weighed my little bag of money in my overalls' pocket.

"He swore it up and down. You can ask Mack. Me and Mack went by ourselves. He swore it worked and he told us the very time, the one time of the year that it worked." Georgie squatted, just at my sisters' eye-level. He looked deadly serious. Susie and Sissy didn't blink.

"When is the very time?" I asked.

"Tomorrow night, that's what he said. He the carnival'd be over in Whittier then, so he could find the perfect spot to bury his money. It's got to be close to water and to a big oak. Not just anyplace will do. Graveyards is best, he said. But old oaks and pure water's the next best thing. I'll tell you something—" He stopped and shook his head.

We waited. My little bag didn't seem quite so heavy now.

"I'll tell you what," Georgie said. "I'm a-gonna bury my money. I don't see how in the world I can lose. The world's oldest man swore he'd seen it happen, and I'm a-gonna try it. I expect I'll be rich in a year or two." He stood up and dusted off his hands on his pants.

"Can we bury ours too?" Sissy asked.

Susie chimed in, "I want to be rich too."

"Well," Georgie said, "I don't know. It's yours, not mine to say."

Susie and Sissy turned to me, their older sister at age seven and a half. I jiggled the bag of coins in my pocket. It was a temptation to think my money would grow. I knew—knew it would not, but it was a mighty temptation to think it might.

"That old man, I mean he's the oldest man in the world, that's what the carnival said, he swore it worked. And I, for one, am bound to try it." Georgie started to walk away, then looked back. "It's got to be done tomorrow night, not a day later. I know the exact spot. I've already thought about it."

"Where, where?" my sisters whispered.

"Well, naturally, I ain't telling you where, not unless you're with me. I've checked, though, and I know the certain spot. Got to be done tomorrow, not a minute later than thirty-seven minutes past seven, that's what he said, and not a minute sooner than seventeen minutes past seven. Sevens is special. It's got to be when the moon and stars is lined up exactly."

My sisters just knew we'd be rich. Our money bags would grow—somehow; some magic was in the air, in the oak and water. I wanted to believe.

The next night we scurried behind Georgie through a field and up to an abandoned well, territory forbidden to us. The old well was overgrown with honeysuckle vines, and wild rose bushes surrounded it. At different times, someone concerned with the safety of children or drunks would put boards over its opening. They rotted and sank inward. Within a few yards stood a huge oak, dripping leaves and acorns.

With ceremony, Georgie determined the exact spot where his money bag was to be planted. Susie, Sissy, and I chose spots close to his, sure that if his crop was plentiful, so would ours be. Georgie used a short-handled shovel for his work; with a trowel and two spoons, we three followed his instructions and dug just as he had. We placed our cloth bags with the coins in the shallow holes.

"You don't want them too deep," Georgie said. "Seeds too deep don't do so well."

That made sense. We scooped little mounds of soft dirt over the three money plots. Each one of us found a twig or rock and marked our spot. "You don't want to take any chances on getting them mixed up," Georgie said. Satisfied with our investment, we trooped back home. My pocket really felt light without its eighteen cents, but I was excited about the possibility, the assurance, of seeing our money grow. I could not quite imagine it, so I stopped trying. After all, Mama had declared one day, "Child, you let your imagination run away with you half the time."

So I just believed.

We mentioned our money plots to each other every day and checked on our "gardens" whenever we could sneak off from Mama and the baby. We even watered them one day when no rain had fallen in over two weeks. "This water may not help a bit," Susie declared. "It's not from the well."

"It's pure, though," I told her. "It's from Jasper's branch, straight up the mountain." Still, I wondered. And I missed the heaviness of the coins in my pocket. I thought and thought about just how that money could grow. I wanted to ask Daddy, but he was always tired or had his eyes set on something over my head.

"Let's go check on our money," I said. I saw Georgie, who had been working at his uncle's for three weeks, coming around the corner of the house. "We're worried," I told him.

"Why, that money's not going to come up just like that," he said. "It's heavier than ordinary seeds. It's bound to take longer."

"We're going anyway."

Georgie came with us. We walked carefully around the mounds that looked like little graves for birds. It looked like the forked stick on my plot had been moved, but I couldn't be sure. I said, "I'm going to dig down and see if anything's happening." It seemed to me Georgie wasn't taking us seriously. He had a halfway grin on his squinty-eyed face.

While Georgie stood there, we set to it with sharp sticks and our hands, digging down three inches or so. I knew it before I saw it for sure: my plot was empty. No coins. No bag. Sissy and Susie found the same thing. Nothing. Sissy started bawling. She cried even louder when Susie said, "Some old witch probably come by and dug it up."

"Well, that old man never said it'd just disappear." Georgie scratched his head. I stared at him. Susie jabbed her stick in Georgie's plot and started digging.

"Hey, leave mine alone. It's likely sprouting this very minute." Georgie grabbed Susie's hand but she scraped off the dirt. There was his little leather pouch. Sissy kept crying. Susie and I eyed the pouch.

"Guess maybe it's just gonna work for men," Georgie declared. With his foot he covered the hole again. "I've got to get on home. You better come with me. Your mama'll skin you alive for being up here at this well by yourselves."

Whistling a ragged tune, Georgie swaggered off. We followed, feet dragging. Our money was gone and no old witch had got it.

And the curly-walnut men had left the area.

Roan Mountain

Malcolm Glass

An ocean of pink and fuchsia
spreads across Roan Mountain,
undulant waves of clustered
blooms of rhododendron, known
to many as mountain laurel.

A hard, determined wind ruffles
and blurs lavender and rose
across the dense green leaves
of bushes twelve or more feet high.

Underneath, spindly bare limbs
twist skyward, pushing foliage
and flowers to the sun and building
below a skeleton and clear ground
flecked with nodding patches of light.

In this labyrinth of bones, the hells,
bears spearhead trails, as they shoulder
and pad their way through the shadows
at the bottom of the dazzling sea.

The Greatest Everything But

Neth Williams

He was the guy anyone could turn to at any time.
He had a terminal disease;
the need to please.
His shoulders were soaked from the tears of mankind.
He was paid in praise;
It charged him for days.
At the drop of a hat, he was gone to console.
While I sat alone;
Crying at home.
He was the greatest of all in a therapist role.
But not to me;
Never for me.

All who needed a hand needed only to call.
Available on demand;
Previous plans be damned.
Travel plans and dinner dates started to fall.
None of that mattered;
Relationships tattered.
Strangers' obligations were first on the poll.
Home only to rest;
After others got his best.
He was the greatest of all in a supporting role.
But not to me;
Never for me.

He could motivate the downtrodden to carry on.
Help them dig deep;
Put worries to sleep.
Staying with many people until the break of dawn.
Ignoring the home;
Leaving me alone.
He would help strangers at the expense of his soul.
Taking on their pain;
Letting himself drain.
He was the greatest of all in a motivating role.
But not to me;
Never for me.

He was the greatest everything to everyone.
A call away;
To save the day.
He would put in hours until the job was done.
Overexerting;
Always hurting.
Everyone in town was better off, so what?
I paid the price;
For him being nice.
He was the greatest everything, but
But not to me;
Never for me.

Some Things You Don't Talk About

Micah Ward

I was nine years old that summer when the thunderstorms rolled in most every afternoon and this story began. I am fifty this gray winter of the big snow as the story comes to its end. These are the things that happened in between.

"Look at that, I pissed all the way out over the boxwoods and hit the mimosa tree!" I was standing on Grandma's wooden porch with my cousins Eli and Teddy and we were seeing who could pee the longest distance out into the yard.

"That ain't nothin'. Watch me piss on that damned ol' hound dawg," shouted Eli.

And with that proclamation, Eli aimed over the steps and rained down a steady stream on our grandpa's old blue tick hound. The hound stood up, stretched, flapped his ears, and walked off to collapse in the sparse shade of the mimosa tree.

"You best quit that cussin' Eli," said Teddy. "I'll tell Grandma and I might just tell Grandpa that you peed on his dawg too."

Eli, who was nine years old, turned on his younger brother holding up a fist with one hand while his other still held on to his tiny little pecker. "I'll box your jaws if you say a damned word Teddy, you hear me?"

The two of them glared at each other, ready to fight. Then a simultaneous flash of lightning and explosion of thunder grabbed their attention. Fat drops of rain began to dot the dirt patches in the yard. Grandpa's hound made it onto the porch just as the next clap of thunder rolled through and the sky dumped sheets of rain down on the length of Goshen Ridge. The storms blew from the west and the thunder rolled down the valley, trapped between Goshen Ridge, where we lived, and Bald Knob which sat a few miles south of us.

The brothers' desire to fight seemed to wash away with the rain as we retreated from the edge of the porch and sat with our backs to the wall of the house. The wind blew mists of rain across the porch from time to time and we hugged our knees to our chests and laughed in the coolness. Breathing in that unique smell of fresh rain.

The screen door opened and our grandfather walked onto the porch. He was the oldest man in the world. At least, to us he was. After stepping out of the door he swung a white cane around to hit the wall and then followed the wall with his hand until the cane located his rocking chair. Grandpa was blind as a bat. He was also tall and thin and had an explosion of sparse white hair that stuck out in all directions. His handlebar mustache was white as snow and covered his entire mouth. He settled into his chair and Eli asked, "You think it's gonna rain all day Grandpa?"

"No, don't reckon it will," he replied. "Rain this hard don't last too long. If'n it was rainin' real light then it could go on all day."

"Will it quit in time for us to go down to the Blue Springs?" Eli asked.

"I suppose it might," Grandpa answered. "But it don't matter none. Ain't nobody goin' down there 'til Saturday anyways."

Both Grandpa and Eli had to shout to be heard above the noise of the rain beating on the tin roof and the thunder that continued to roll down through the valley. Hoover, the blue tick hound, walked over to Grandpa's chair and laid his head on the old man's lap. Grandpa rubbed Hoover's head and Teddy couldn't hold it in any longer.

"Hoover needs to go down to the river and wash off 'cause Eli peed on him!"

Grandpa just kept on rocking and rubbing Hoover's head and asked in a softer voice, "Now Eli, why did you want to go and do a thing like that for?"

The storm eventually blew off and the rain ended by the time Grandma called us in for supper. We took our places around the enormous table with Grandma and Grandpa and our uncle Clarence. He was one of my momma's seven brothers and had never married. He was a thin man like Grandpa. But where Grandpa was calm and relaxed, Clarence constantly shifted his eyes and seemed to quiver with a contained nervousness.

Clarence had moved in with Grandma and Grandpa when he came back from the war and never left. Looking over his shoulder I saw the framed newspaper article about Clarence and the other brothers that Grandma kept on an antique table there in the dining room. Some of the brothers fought the Japanese in the big war and some the Germans. They all lived through it and when they came home the town folk made a big deal out of it. I didn't really understand it until I got a lot older and studied up on that war.

We were seated at the table passing the food around after grace had been said and Teddy whispered to Clarence, "Eli pissed on Hoover."

"Quiet now!" Grandpa boomed, "You young'uns know you ain't allowed talk at the table. That's for grownups."

"The proper word is urinated, Teddy," said Grandma. "After supper you will sit down with pencil and paper and I will show you how to write it. Then you will write it one hundred times and you will never say piss in my presence again."

Teddy hung his head and muttered, "Yes ma'am."

Clarence grinned and winked at me and Eli. The we ate in silence while the adults talked about adult things. Grandpa had to lift his mustache out of the way when he drank his buttermilk and

Clarence would grin and wink at us. But we kept our giggles silent and Grandma pretended not to notice.

After supper my cousins and I always helped Grandma carry the plates and bowls, glasses, and whatnot from the table into the kitchen. She then piled food onto a big plate and covered it with wax paper. I knew what was coming but before I could get out of the kitchen she said, "Come on little Henry, let's take this plate over to Chief."

Chief was a cousin of some sort and lived in a little two room shack next to Grandma and Grandpa's house. He was in the big war too and Clarence said that Chief had been in Patton's army at the Battle of the Bulge. Chief never said if he was or wasn't. In fact, nobody to my knowledge ever heard him say anything after he returned from the war.

I remember one of the last times I went with her to take food to Chief. I followed Grandma with her tall straight back and purposeful steps as we walked along the narrow well beaten path around the garden. She knocked on the door of Chief's shack. "Evenin' Chief, little Henry and I brought you supper."

I could hear the floor creak with Chief's footsteps before the door opened. Chief was short and husky and had hair that was shiny black like a raven. He nodded at Grandma as he took the plate of food and then looked down at me with a face devoid of expression. I'm not sure why but I was always a little afraid of Chief.

"You need anything else Chief?" Grandma asked.

He shook his head and reached out his hand to pat Grandma on the shoulder. I snuck a peek at the disheveled furniture and dim light of Chief's living quarters and it just added to the general fear I had of that man.

"Well, you come over for breakfast in the mornin' if you like. The kitchen window'll be open and when you smell the bacon fryin' just come in and join us."

Chief nodded his head and turned to retreat into his shack. As we walked back along the bare earth of the path, I asked Grandma, "Why do you always invite Chief to breakfast? He don't ever come."

"It's the Christian thing to do Henry. Always extend a helpin' hand to people even if you know they won't take it. And you should say doesn't and not don't in that sentence."

"Yes ma'am." In addition to being a Christian, Grandma was a school teacher and very particular about how we boys talked.

Eli, Teddy, and I were spending the summer with our grandparents. All our families lived in the same community so it wasn't such a big thing. Our parents were only five miles or so away but it was a major adventure for children our age.

I slept in the same room with uncle Clarence in a pair of old sagging twin beds that almost filled the room. Most nights he tossed around in the bed and made noises that weren't quite yelling and weren't quite crying. Even though I was only nine, I had heard stories about the war and guessed that Clarence was fighting the Japs again in his sleep.

I asked my dad about him and the uncles and how they all went to war and none of them were killed. My father's explanation was simple enough, "I got lucky. But your momma's brothers are too damn mean to get killed in a war. Why, they's the ones doin' most of the killin'."

But none of my uncles were ever mean to me or Eli or Teddy. One of them was Eli and Teddy's old man and he never even whipped those boys. My father was a waist gunner in a B-17 and he came back from the war. Does that mean he did a lot of killing too? Was he mean like my uncles? I studied on that question for a lot of years and I asked him a few days before he died. He just said that there are some things you don't talk about. I never thought he was a mean man but he was right about those things that were better left unsaid. I learned that myself that very same summer.

Saturdays were the best days of summer because that's when we would go to the Blue Springs River. The river was about twenty-five yards across and there was a sandy beach on one side and a wall of rocks on the other. Oak trees gave us both shade and limbs to hang swings on. My parents would come for the day along with all the other uncles and their wives and kids. Car loads of chairs, fishing tackle, food, and blankets for the ground.

The children swarmed the beach, swam from one side of the river to the other and jumped off rocks and limbs into the slow crawling water. The men ranged the river above the swimming hole to fish and below the hole to pull in trot lines dangling with catfish. They all drank homemade wine, the women sipping discretely as it was done in those days. And they all shared the gossip and town rumors while Grandpa managed to work a condemnation of the Republicans into almost every conversation.

Chief sat off by himself and stared out at the river. Looking at whatever it was he saw in the distance over the water.

There was a ring of blackened rocks on the beach where the fire was built every Saturday to cook the days catch. Shortly after dark the women would round up the children and return to their homes. The men settled in around the fire and spent the night at the river with a seemingly inexhaustible supply of the homemade wine. I always wondered what was so great about the river after dark that my dad and uncles would stay there all night.

I picked the wrong night to find out.

The Blue Springs River was only a twenty-minute walk from Grandma's house; even for little guys like Eli, Teddy, and me. In fact, we had snuck off a couple of times that summer and walked to the river for a quick skinny dip. We were never gone for more than a couple of hours and in those days, nobody worried about boys roaming the fields and forests around a grandparent's house. So, it wasn't really a big deal when I proposed to Eli that we sneak back out to the river one Saturday night to see what the men were doing.

"We don't need to take Teddy with us. He's liable to tell somebody," Eli said.

"That's right; he's too young and he can't keep a secret. We'll wait until he falls asleep then you sneak into my room and we'll go."

"Yeah, we'll just go long enough to see what they're doin' then get on back. As long as we make it back by daylight then we'll be in bed when Grandma starts wakin' us up to go to church."

We nearly busted open that week from the pent-up excitement of our secret. It was worse than waiting on Christmas. Our parents and the other families showed up on Saturday as usual and we all piled into pickup trucks and cars for the ride to the Blue Springs.

It was another normal Saturday at the river. We swam and jumped off the rocks and generally did what kids did on summer afternoons. It was hot and sunny and we managed to dodge the afternoon storms that blow through in that time of year.

The men cleaned the fish and cooked them over the fire while the women set out the side dishes. Chief and Grandpa sat alone and apart from the others that day. Now that was a pair; a man who wouldn't talk and a man who couldn't see. But they seemed content enough. Especially since they each had a bottle of that homemade muscadine wine.

It was almost dark when the aunts and mothers and Grandma gathered up all the kids and left the men to the river. Soon after we got back to Grandma's she shuffled us off to bed. I lay there in the twin bed with my clothes on waiting for Eli to come. Listening to the ticking of the big grandfather clock and smelling the ever-present aroma of the slop pot under the bed. I half expected Eli to fall asleep and not show up but just as the big clock in the living room chimed eleven times, he tiptoed through the door.

We slipped out of the house and luckily had a full moon to light the way for us. An owl hooted off in the distance and crickets chirped in the grass. We passed a pond and the bass croak of bull-frogs drowned out all the other night noises. We walked along the dirt road that led down to the river full of ourselves and the adventure we had taken on. Two boys of nine years each strutting with the bravado that only the clueless possess. And we believed that we would see something strange and magical at our destination.

We slowed down and became more cautious when we stepped off the main road and onto the single lane path that led to the river. We crept halfway to where the pickups were parked and then slipped into the trees on the side of the trail. Drawn as creatures are toward the light of the fire. We figured the sound of our approach would be covered by the croaks of the bullfrogs at the river.

"Grandpa has Hoover down here. You think he'll bark at us," I whispered.

"I don't think so, that damned old dawg don't bark at nothin'. He probably won't even know we're here."

We crept in close and hid behind a fallen tree. We could see the beach area lit from bushes to water. The fire was burning large and casting dancing shadows against the surrounding brush. My dad and all seven uncles were sitting around the flames. Grandpa was also in the circle with Hoover lying at his feet and off to one side Chief sat on a stump and stared out into the distance. They passed around bottles of the homemade wine and talked softly among themselves. Every so often one of them would say something that made them all laugh. And sometimes they would all just nod their heads and go silent for a minute or two. Obviously contemplating some truth beyond the understanding of mere boys. Since we were still too far away to hear those truths, Eli nudged my arm and whispered, "You think we ought to try to get closer?"

Before I could answer we heard another sound that neither of us had expected. The sound of a vehicle with a loud muffler. It came down the lane toward the river beach. We looked back and were blinded by the lights shining down the track as the vehicle approached. It passed and we saw that it was a large four door sedan. It came to a stop and the doors opened and six large shapes in white robes and tall conical white hats emerged.

"Sonofabitch," Eli exclaimed. "It's the goddamned Ku Klux Klan."

I felt a warm wetness in the front of my pants as I peed on myself.

The Klansmen walked toward the fire and formed a circle around the men of our family. None of my uncles or my dad gave any indication that they even noticed their arrival. Hoover sat up and Grandpa put his hands on the dog's shoulders. I glanced at Chief and saw him look in the direction of the fire then turn his gaze back toward the dark.

There was no wind but the crickets and frogs were loud and when one of the Klansmen started talking, we realized we were too far away to hear. Scared though we were, Eli and I slipped along the length of the fallen tree and into a shallow ditch. We followed the ditch toward the fire until we could hear one of the Klansman speaking. He seemed to be addressing my uncle George. Eli and Teddy's old man.

"Now it ain't right for you to have a colored boy workin' for you when they's lots of white men who need jobs around here."

I realized that he had to be talking about Rudolf. George ran a brick laying crew and Rudolf was a Black man that worked for him. Nobody knew all the details but George and Rudolf had known each other in the war and when George started his crew, he hired Rudolf.

George spit tobacco juice into the fire and looked sideways up at the Klansman. "Just who the hell do you think you are comin' down here at this time of night and tellin' me who to hire and who not to hire? I've known Rudolf a long time and he does good work and I'll have him workin' for me as long as he wants to."

"You just don't understand the proper order of things," said the Klansman. "We got to take care of the white folks first. Now the Klan is powerful around here and we don't mind takin' things into our hands if we have to. We got night riders that can put up a burnin' cross in no time. We'll run that colored boy plumb out of the county if we got to and once we burn a cross on your yard and all them damn brothers of yours they won't be anybody within a hundred miles that'll hire you."

Up until now my daddy and uncles and grandpa had just sat around the fire staring at the flames in silence. But then they all straightened their backs and looked at the six Klansmen standing arrogantly in the firelight with hands on hips or arms crossed across chest.

Grandpa's voice boomed out over the beach, "You stupid sonsabitches have come pickin' a fight with the wrong people. I've knowed your kind for years and I ain't no more impressed with you now than I was when your daddies was ridin' horses in those same damned silly assed sheets. You better get the hell on out of here and I mean right now. We ain't gonna pay any more attention to you than we would two mules fightin' over a turnip."

Daddy and the uncles laughed in agreement with Grandpa's proclamation and the Klansmen shifted their feet and posture in an attitude of increased belligerence. The main one pointed his finger at Grandpa and started shouting something about proper respect for the defenders of the white race.

That's when I saw Chief walking silently out of the shadows.

Chief straightened his arm and pointed something small and black toward the back of the Klansman's head and there was a soft popping sound. The Klansman collapsed in a disjointed mess of arms and legs. Clarence and another uncle named Herbert quickly stood up, their arms extended and they gunned down the rest of the Klansmen before any could react.

Dad, Grandpa, and the other uncles never stood up. They simply looked around at the bodies on the ground and then Dad looked toward Grandpa and said, "Mr. Schneider, your boys just shot the shit out of the Ku Klux Klan."

There was silence for a second. Then they all broke out into uncontrollable laughter. A laughter that seemed so wrong in such a situation that to this day it is still the scariest thing I've ever heard.

Eli started to shake and began to cry. I wrapped one arm around his shoulders and put my hand over his mouth and whispered, "Quiet, Eli. Don't let 'em hear us. We'll be in bad trouble."

We laid there in the ditch for what seemed like hours. My father, Eli's father, Grandpa, our uncles, and Chief; the men of our family, our role models and heroes; simply sat around the fire sipping wine and talking in low murmurs as if the six dead bodies lying there beside them were of no consequence at all. Eventually, they drug the bodies of the dead Klansmen over to their sedan and stuffed them into the trunk and back seat. Clarence and George got into the sedan and turned it around and headed back down the lane toward the main road. The rest of the men climbed into the remaining trucks and followed the sedan out.

Eli and I ran all the way back to Grandma's house.

The men returned to the house around the same time as the women and children returned from church. The women prepared dinner and we kids changed out of our church clothes and into playing clothes. It was like any other summer Sunday. But for two of us it was like no other Sunday would ever be again. I might as well of dreamed the events of the night before. No one acted differently. The men may have been a little quieter than normal and the women probably attributed that to hangovers from too much wine. It was as if Eli and I were the only ones aware of an earth changing secret. We made eye contact from time to time but neither of us said a word.

For the next few days, it was harder for us to take any pleasure in our peeing contests or anything else. At random times, Eli and I looked at each other but neither of us spoke a word about what we had seen. I think both of us were waiting on the other to say something and neither of us was willing to be the first to bring it up. We noticed that Grandpa and Chief spent more time sitting under a big shade tree together. Clarence joined them when he came in from work in the afternoons and we instinctively knew that we should leave them alone.

It was Wednesday, after two days of hard rain, when the Sheriff showed up and talked to Grandpa and Clarence. He wanted to talk to Chief too, but Chief never talked to anyone so the Sheriff didn't make much progress with him.

The Sheriff squeezed his enormous rear end into one of the rocking chairs on the front porch. Grandpa and Clarence occupied theirs with calm indifference. Eli and Teddy and I crouched in the boxwoods off one end of the porch so that we could hear what was said. Of course, we hadn't told Teddy anything about what was going on. He just thought it was fun to eavesdrop on the adults.

Before the Sheriff could really begin his questions, Grandma came to the door. "Will you be stayin' for supper Sheriff Glover?"

"Uh, no ma'am, Mrs. Schneider. The missus' has been boilin' down greens all day so I expect I'll go home for supper."

"Alright then, you tell Maude I said hello," and with that Grandma retreated back into thc house.

"Our greens came in real good this year," Grandpa said. "How was your crop, Sheriff?"

"Oh, we did real good too. This is a fine time of year for greens. Of course, greens ain't what I'm here to talk to you about."

We heard Grandpa spit tobacco juice over the porch into the boxwoods and then ask the Sheriff, "What you got on your mind?"

"Well, this here is what I got on my mind. They's six men from down around Bald Knob missin.' They left home Saturday night and ain't been seen since. Their car ain't been found either. The wives of a couple of them said they was coming down to the river Saturday night to talk to you and your boys."

The Sheriff let that statement hang in the air. A hot, windless air. Finally, Grandpa said, "They was several fellers drove up late when we was sittin' around the fire. Of course, being blind I couldn't tell you how many or if they was from Bald Knob or not. I don't reckon I know too many people from those parts. You were there Clarence, what do you remember?"

"There was about a half dozen of 'em," Clarence said. "I didn't know who they were but they talked to George about some brick layin' work. Didn't stay too long though. They were drinkin' shine and it seemed like they may have drunk a lot of it. A couple of 'em were kind of wobbly if you know what I mean."

"Did they argue with George or anyone else," the Sheriff asked.

"No," Clarence replied. "They just stayed a few minutes. They all piled into a big old sedan of some kind. I do remember that one of the wobbly ones was the driver and I thought to myself, now they gonna wind up in a ditch if he's doing the drivin'. But they didn't wreck goin' back toward the road. Who knows what happened after that?"

The talking paused and was replaced by the back and forth of the rails on the rocking chairs. Grandpa spat tobacco juice again and the Sheriff said, "A couple of those men were pretty big in the Klan."

"I wouldn't know," Grandpa said.

"Me neither," Clarence agreed.

The Sheriff stayed long enough to discuss the weather and fertilizer prices with Grandpa and Clarence. Discussing those mundane topics as if six missing men had never been mentioned. Then he left.

He never came back to talk about the missing Klansmen from Bald Knob as far as I know. But I suppose he talked to George because the next day George came by the house for lunch and had a quiet conversation with Grandpa under that shade tree in the yard. Rudolph sat in the back of George's work truck the whole time. Grandma, ever the fine Christian lady, sent him a plate of food and when Teddy handed it to him, Rudolph just smiled and said thanks. But he stayed in the truck until George drove off.

The rest of the summer passed and Eli and I lived in the cloud of our memories and the reality of our silence. Our Saturday trips to the river lost their childhood innocence. While everyone else carried on as usual I snuck glances at the ring of blackened rocks and wondered why they still looked so normal.

I tried once to talk to Eli about what we saw but he refused to speak of it. So, I kept it inside. And every Saturday I watched my dad and my uncles and my grandpa carry on as if nothing had happened that night when Eli and I hid in the ditch and watched them murder six men. Chief kept his own silent counsel on his stump watching his own procession of ghosts out over the river.

Eli and I never spent another summer at our grandparent's house. We visited with our families and occasionally spent a weekend but never the whole summer. And the more we stayed silent the more it seemed that we would remain that way. After all, who would we tell?

Eli became more withdrawn and he and I grew further apart. As we progressed through high school, he became one of those anonymous students walking largely unnoticed from class to class. No one really disliked him, but at the same time, no one was his close friend. He kept his own counsel, attended classes and had very little to say. When he graduated, he joined the Navy. He said he wanted to learn a skill and see some faraway places before coming back home. But as everyone congratulated him for his maturity and foresight, I knew better. Eli would never come home. This was his escape from that night at the river. After joining the Navy, Eli only visited Beulah Bluff about once a year.

I followed a different path. While Eli withdrew and became a loner, I worked myself into exhaustion with sports. I was a good, but not great, athlete. I was never a star but I worked hard enough to earn starting spots on the football, basketball, and baseball teams. In our own ways we found the means to keep our minds off the Blue Springs River. A small college just outside of Atlanta invited me to play baseball and after graduation I stayed in those ever- expanding suburbs. I married a girl from those suburbs and a couple children came along shortly thereafter. I taught school and coached several sports. It was my way of keeping busy and always having an excuse not to visit Beulah Bluff any more than necessary.

Maybe it was karma or poetic justice. A bit of irony or a random coincidence. But on a late summer day between the end of high school baseball season and the start of football practice I was in Beulah Bluff visiting my grandparents. Grandma seemed as strong as always but Grandpa was confined to a wheelchair and mostly sat in silence.

We were on the porch, rocking slowly in the mugginess and still air. Not a lot of conversation, just enjoying the presence of each other. A dust trail progressed up the long drive and a sheriff's patrol car pulled up. My cousin Teddy stepped out of the car and slowly walked up toward the porch in his starched and pressed uniform and shiny badge. Just the year before, Teddy had been elected sheriff of Graham County.

"My grandson the sheriff, how are you doin' today?" Grandma asked.

"I'm doin' just fine. Howdy Grandpa. Howdy Henry, what brings you up from the big city?"

I looked at my cousin Teddy, the duly elected sheriff, and my mind flashed back to the scene of six Ku Klux Klansmen lying dead on the beach of the Blue Springs River. It always did and it always had, ever since Teddy first put on the uniform of the Sheriff's Department right after he graduated college.

"Oh, I just thought I'd come visit a few people before football season starts. We got two a day practice startin' next Monday and I won't have much free time after that until the end of the season."

Teddy eased himself into a rocking chair, "Gonna have a good team this year?"

"We should have a winnin' season. If we get to the playoffs and win one game, I'll be happy."

"Well, that'll be better than what Graham High is expectin'. They'll do good to win three or four this year. But aside from football I got some interestin' news."

"Is Brenda pregnant again?" Grandma asked.

"Oh no, nothin' that excitin', I think three young'uns is enough for us. No, the big news today has to do with somethin' we found in the river."

It was a hot day. The kind that only exists in the south when the summer holds on as long as possible. A wet blanket of humidity and no breeze. I was damp with sweat but when Teddy mentioned finding something in the river a cold chill ran through me. Then I sweated heavier. Grandpa seemed to be asleep in his wheelchair but he straightened up at Teddy's words.

"What on earth did you find in the river?" asked Grandma.

"Well, I didn't find it," said Teddy. "A couple of boys were floatin' down the river on inner tubes and came up on a car in the water. You know how low the river is right now, what with the drought bein' so bad. I guess it's down a good seven or eight foot or more below Goose Landin'. And these boys noticed the top of a car stickin' up out of the water. So, they called it in and when we pulled that thing up out of the water, you'll never guess what we found."

"You found Elvis," grunted Grandpa.

Grandma laughed out loud, not so much at what Grandpa said but with relief that he could follow and contribute to the conversation. Teddy laughed as well and I forced a smile and a slight chuckle just to be polite. I knew what was likely to be in that car and it damn sure wasn't Elvis.

"Do you remember back about forty years ago when those Ku Klux Klan guys from Bald Knob went missing?" Teddy asked. "Well, I think we found them."

"You don't say," Grandma replied.

"Yep, the car in the river was a 1951 Chevrolet and there were six skeletons in it. The funny thing is that three of them were in the trunk. The coroner examined one of the skulls and it looked like there was a bullet hole in it. We looked at all the others and each one had a similar hole. Of course, I can't say for sure but even with skulls that old, the medical examiner ought to be able to tell if those holes are gunshots."

"Well, I declare," said Grandma as she reached over and patted Grandpa on the leg. "What do you think of that dear?"

This time Grandpa just grunted and Grandma looked dismayed that he had seemingly lost his ability to follow the conversation so quickly.

Teddy looked down at his lap and folded hands and grew serious. "You know Grandma; there was always talk that those boys came down to the river to see Grandpa and the other men the night they disappeared."

"Well, I do believe they mentioned it and Clarence said the whole bunch drove off drunk. That's the way it was and don't you go makin' more of it than that Teddy. You hear me? Now I got to get Grandpa inside. He's gettin' tired."

With that Grandma ended all talk of skeletons in the river. She supervised Teddy and I as we wheeled the old man into the house and then helped him into his bed. We said our goodbyes to Grandma and walked out of the house toward our cars through the dry dusty dirt of the driveway. Teddy stopped and looked back at the old shack where Chief still lived.

"I don't suppose it would do any good to try to talk to Chief and see if he remembers anything about that night. What do you think Henry?"

"I think Chief hasn't said a word to anybody since 1945 and I don't think he's goin' to change that now."

It was a few weeks later. Football practice had ended and players and coaches shambled slowly across the field toward the locker rooms. The first cool breezes that announce autumn surrounded me as I trailed behind them. A familiar figure sat in the bleachers. I climbed up the steps and sat down beside him.

"What do you think Cousin Sheriff? Are we goin' to be any good?"

"I think your quarterback is a little slow on his release."

"I've been thinkin' the same thing. So, what in the world are you doin' down this way?"

"I had to run some errands at the State Crime Lab so I thought I would drop by to say hello. Unfortunately, I got some bad news. Have you talked to anyone from Beulah Bluff today?"

"No," I said with apprehension. "I left my phone in the locker room. What's goin' on?"

"Grandma went out to Chief's shack around lunchtime and found him dead."

"Well, I'll be. How old was Chief, around 90 or so?"

"Yeah, I guess so. Grandpa won't last much longer either. He's even worse now than when you last saw him."

"It's hard to believe. It seems like he's been old as long as I can remember. Our dads are gone, now Chief's gone and Grandpa's almost there. They're all just fadin' away."

"Yeah, they are," sighed Teddy and then his demeanor changed. It was something akin to a shift in the breeze, subtle but just enough to be noticed. "Only three of the ones that were on the Blue Springs River the night those men disappeared are still livin'. When Grandpa passes it'll just be uncle Clarence and uncle Herbert and he doesn't even remember his own name anymore."

I sat there in silence with a vivid memory of what I saw on the river on a night forty years before. In the distance the first of the red and orange leaves fell from trees and scattered across campus.

"And what if they did," I asked. "Are you thinkin' our dads and uncles had anything to do with anything? And if they did, what would you do?"

"I don't know Henry. I just don't know. All six of those men were shot in the head, some in the back and some right in the face. You know how our dads and uncles were bad to carry pistols with them. I just can't help but wonder about it."

Teddy shifted around on the bleacher and looked right at me. "I emailed Eli the other day and told him about findin' the car and the bodies. He wrote me back and said to leave it alone. And the curious thing is that he told me not to talk to you about it either. He said they's some things you just don't talk about and left it at that. What do you reckon he meant?"

"Don't know," I said. "But I better get on into the locker room before those knuckleheads destroy it. Good to see you again Teddy. I'll see you at Chief's funeral."

I walked to the end of the practice field and just before going into the field house I looked back. Teddy was still sitting on the bleachers watching me, the low setting sun turning him into a silhouette.

A new snowfall is a beautiful sight. I stood at our sliding glass doors sipping coffee and looking at the snow that had accumulated the night before. The sky was gray and the wind was still and there were no footprints yet to spoil the smooth white landscape that stretched across the backyard and into the woods.

I had just hung up the phone after listening to Teddy deliver the news of Grandpa's death. The old man had lasted longer than we expected. Through the football season and most of basketball season and long enough to celebrate he and Grandma's 80th wedding anniversary. Although he didn't really know what was going on. And now the old man was gone.

A new snowfall is indeed a beautiful sight. But five inches of fresh snow between Atlanta and Beulah Bluff is hard to navigate. Even with four-wheel drive. Our normal two-hour journey was doubled and we made it to Grandma's house just as Teddy and Clarence brought her back from the funeral home. It had not taken long to make the plans for Grandpa's funeral. It would be short and to the point.

Several women from the family were ministering to Grandma while others gathered the wet and snowy coats, hats and boots as people arrived. Other women ferried a steady stream of food into the dining room. In the south, people may not know what to say at the time of a death so they bring food. Lots of food. I followed a cousin that I barely remembered into the dining room and was enveloped by the aromas of fried chicken, baked ham, casseroles, biscuits, cornbread and most any type of cake and pie that you can imagine.

The house was filled with the low murmur of conversations that attend the time of dying. I weaved through relatives, friends and strangers and found Clarence sitting alone in his room. I sat down on the twin bed where I used to listen to Clarence fight the war in his sleep and patted my old uncle on the knee.

"You doin' ok?" I asked.

"I woke up about seven," Clarence said. "When I got to the kitchen, I noticed the coffee wasn't percolatin' so I walked down to their room and looked in. Momma was sittin' there in her night shirt holdin' his hand and singin' Rock of Ages. When she saw me, she just shook her head and looked back down at him. She ain't said a word since."

And Grandma would never say another word. Ever. We got through Grandpa's funeral, and the day after, Grandma did not get out of bed. Clarence and a few of the women relatives, including my wife Nellie, tended to her. Propped on thick pillows and covered with hand quilted covers she would stare into space as if no one else was there. They took her soup and read to her from the Bible. And on the seventh night after Grandpa died, Grandma followed him.

I pondered the nature of Chief's silence. What could he have seen or done or have done to him that he never spoke again after coming home from the war? I pondered Grandma's silence. She and Grandpa married when they were sixteen years old and spent eighty years together. Were those seven days after Grandpa died the worst of her life? Were they so bad that silence was the only way of dealing with them? Was that the nature of Chief's silence? Was it the only way to deal with something so bad that he just couldn't talk about it or anything else? Grandma always seemed to understand Chief.

Two days later we buried Grandma. I stood by Eli as we both gazed at the grave stoves. He looked good in his Navy uniform, blue with gold adornments and multicolored ribbons.

"You want to talk about it?" I asked.

"Talk about what?"

Eli didn't wait for me to answer. He turned and quietly walked off through the field of gravestones past the bare trees to the waiting car.

Years have passed since Grandma's funeral and I no longer ponder silence. I am silence. Silent about what I saw on a summer night by the Blue Springs River.

Addy's Gift

Hubert Blair Bonds

Mazeppa, Iredell County, North Carolina
March 30, 1863

Mama always said that I had gotten it from her grandmother. "You got the gift that my Grandma had, little gal." I only knew it to be a sick feeling that sometimes gnawed away at my stomach.

And sometimes it started with a twitching in my left eye. She'd say, "Addy McNeely, you got the same power that Grandma Denny had. She come here right from Ireland, and she could see things. And she read tea leaves, but she didn't want nobody to know."

I never wanted the power–it was more of a burden than a gift. After I married Will Peacock, it centered around him more than anything or anybody.

"How's about we take a trip next Monday to the General Store? It's time for me to get some seed and you said there were a few things you needed."

Immediately, the gnawing in my stomach began. "I don't really need anything, Will. Not anything that can't wait."

He turned and looked at me, "Which is it this time? The twitchin' or the gnawin'?"

"I'm sorry. It's just the gnawin' so far."

He smiled that smile of his that usually calmed my nerves. "You don't have to say you're sorry. It's part of you, and I like knowin' that there's a part of you that's always lookin' out for me."

"Well, I don't like it. And I don't think that I will ever like it. I wish it had skipped on to somebody besides me."

Monday morning came, and we struck out for the General Store just after daylight. This power was working overtime in me today. The gnawing felt like it was drilling through my stomach and about to flood my gut.

"You never know about a March day. Some are winter, and some are spring. It even smells like spring today," I said as a way of making conversation and calming my insides.

"You're right as rain. That's one reason I wanted to get seeds. I think it will be warm enough by Good Friday to plant."

"Mama always said that Good Friday was the only time to plant. I guess I will start the kitchen garden then too."

"I know you saved seed from last year, but we can get some at the store if you want."

"I will look at them."

It was not a long trip to the General Store, but it gave my stomach the time it needed to settle. The countryside was waking up from the long winter. In some of the sunnier spots, I could tell that the Bleeding Judas trees were about to bust open. They had always been a curiosity to me, the way their gray twigs would suddenly be covered in purplish blooms. In some spots, I could see the dogwood blossoms beginning to turn from pale green to white just before they opened. And the butter-yellow daffodils were poking their heads up and beginning to flower.

"I do believe that spring is my favorite time of year," volunteered Will.

"I didn't think you were noticing. I figured your mind was on seeds and planting and harvesting."

"Well, a little bit, yes. What's your favorite time of year, Addy?"

"You know that I love the autumn time. The trees are all colorful, and the orange pumpkins and gourds. It's the time that you can rest for a bit from all the summer work and enjoy what you've brought forth."

"It's certainly a time of bounty if the seasons cooperate with us."

"There's the store now."

"Do I look alright? You never know who you're going to run into."

"You look fine. You always do."

"Oh, you…you're just a striped sight."

"You're the only person in the world that says that. I don't even know what it means."

"My mama said it. And it means that you're just a mess."

"All right, but can't a man tell his wife that she looks fine?"

"You just stop this wagon and let me get in the store."

A grin spread across Will's face as he pulled the wagon to a stop. "Let me come around and help you down."

The store was empty except for the owner, Ephraim Patterson. "Well, good morning, Will. And Missus Peacock. Always glad to have you here."

"Morning, Mr. Patterson. Will is looking for seed, and I might be as well. Otherwise, I'm just going to be looking around."

"That's fine. You just look to your heart's content."

I looked at the piece goods and saw some nice fabric. "How are you able to keep such nice piece goods, Mr. Patterson? With the Yankees blocking our ports, I'm really surprised."

Mr. Patterson smiled. "It's all local. The calico came from a mill up in Surry County, and the dotted Swiss came from Rowan County."

As lovely as the fabric was, once again, the pit of my stomach was paining. Not much more than an hour's rest from it.

"Mrs. Peacock?"

"I'm sorry, Mr. Patterson. My mind was somewhere else."

"Never you mind. I was just saying I could give you a good price on the calico because it's been here for a bit of time."

"Thank you. I'll think about it."

I walked over to the window with my unruly stomach, hoping the view from there would help it stop. In the distance, I saw a cloud of dirt coming from the south. And I heard something as well. Was it a drum?

Will and Mr. Patterson heard it, too, and joined me at the window just as gray uniforms came into view. The man in front was on a white stallion and had a big yellow plume on his hat. He glanced our way and turned the steed toward the store.

"Have you got your papers, Will?" I asked as the man dismounted.

"Right in my pocket."

The man with the plume entered the store. "Captain Wayne from the 1st North Carolina Cavalry Regiment. Why aren't you men in the service of our cause?"

Mr. Moore said, "I'm the owner of this store, and I was given permission to stay here and keep it open. We're the only store around here."

The Captain nodded and then looked at Will. "And you, sir?"

"My father paid the bond, and another fella went in my place. I have the papers."

"Let me see them."

The papers were already in Will's hand, hanging down at his side. The Captain studied them.

"We need men, Mr. Peacock. You're going to have to come with us. We need you."

"But we paid good money…"

"I understand that. You have no choice."

I knew a woman's place, but that had never stopped me before, and I wasn't about to be shy now.

"Look here, my father-in-law paid in gold for him to not have to go. Did you hear me? I said gold. Not Confederate money."

The Captain turned his stare to me, "Yes, ma'am. I understand that. But that was two years ago. Things have changed. We need more able-bodied men."

"He's not going."

"Ma'am, if I have to put a bayonet in his back and march him all the way to Winston, I will. But it's better for him if he goes with us on his own."

"Will, you can't go. It's been fixed already. Your papers prove it."

"I don't think that bond is worth the paper it is printed on, Addy. If I don't go, Captain, what's the alternative?"

"You'd be considered a prisoner of war, and I'd still have to take you. Do you have a gun in your wagon?"

"Yes, of course."

"Get moving. You can kiss your wife goodbye out there."

"Will! You can't. What am I going to do about the farm?"

"I don't think I have a choice, Addy. I'd rather go like this than spend years in a prison camp. Don't go back to the farm. Stop at my folks, and they will keep you there."

I grabbed Will's arm, trying to keep him inside. The Captain saw and shook his head, "Ma'am, you need to stop interfering."

"Interfering? You, sir, are the one that is interfering in my life, just because you have a uniform on."

"Mr. Peacock, you need to control your wife."

"Addy, calm down. I will talk to his higher-ups when we get to Winston. I'll probably be home by Friday."

"All right, Will. If you're not, I'll bc up there by Monday."

"Out to the wagon, folks," commanded the Captain.

"I have two shotguns. Can my wife keep one? She needs some sort of protection on the road going home."

"From what I've seen of your wife, she can cut a man's heart out with her tongue. But, yes, leave one with her. Tell her goodbye and let's get going."

"I can't believe this. I know now what my gift was trying to tell me the last three days. We should have stayed home."

"They have been going through the countryside taking people. I heard tell of it about two weeks ago."

"And you didn't tell me."

"Addy, calm down. I don't have a choice. He has the power, not me. Kiss me and be on your way to Ma and Pa's."

We embraced and kissed. "Make sure you come back to me, Will Peacock."

"I don't plan on doing anything else."

I watched Will join the others. The Captain tipped his hat my way, "I'm only doing my duty ma'am. I'm sorry."

"And I'll only be doing my duty to get him home again."

"Yes, ma'am. Do what you need to do."

I watched them go down the road until they were out of sight. I felt like my life was walking away with Will. Our dreams were ours. I didn't want them to be just mine. And I didn't want this damned gift anymore. It wasn't a gift, no matter what Mama said. It was a curse. It did me no good. It did Will no good. And now he was gone.

A Kiss Blown in the Mirror

Ann Hite

You were always in the mirror.
Standing, waiting, watching.
You with a goofy grin,
Looking on as if I mattered.

The heart of our life plays out in unison with the seasons,
Moving like a river over rocks, that try to stop us.
But we move too fast, too smooth, too like the wind,
The hawks holding still in the air. High.

We finish each other's thoughts.
Magic. Love. Kindness.
Knowledge of each other's movements
Before we make them.

Knowing our words, thoughts, pains.
We are the kisses in the mirror,
The life in reflection,
In a ripple of glass.

Home is the kisses blown into the air,
The life carved out of raw edges,
Hard times, repaired in the future.
Life in meadows of wildflowers.

A Kiss when we made vows years before.
We hold that kiss in the mirror
Close to our hearts
Close to our skin.

If we had feathers we would move with the
Wind in and out of the treetops.
Wingtips touching,
Flapping in the chill of the air.

If we held hands as young teenagers
Would we be here now? In this world we built
From kisses in the mirror, of music, of pain,
Of kindness, love, a fabric tightly woven.

Years are water flowing in a river, rushing to the ocean.
People leave, die, cry, but still we move in our dance,
Up into the crisp air,
Close to the mountaintop, close to heaven.

Kisses are blown in the mirror where we look at each other's
Reflections, silent,
Braided in this long breath of
Air taken in unison.

HOMEPLACE

Rickie Zayne Ashby

My homeplace is not across the sea
The land is my abode
No search for El Dorado
Seeking in vain
While growing old and lame

I do not destroy
To awaken new dreams
Roads not taken
I do not fret
I heal what I have

Prosper in place
Content with less
For it is more
Not frustrated with futile desires
Nor unrealistic dreams

The land touches my heart
I need not wander
Or stray from home
The land is my abode
I need not exploit

---To fulfill my dreams

Dream Merchant

Francine Rodriguez

She ran over the curb, jarring the steering wheel and twisting her wrist hard as she turned her head away from the street in front of her to look at another new "Black Lives Matter" sign that was stuck in a clump of weeds at the entrance of the school parking lot. Her cup of black coffee with diet sweetener splashed with the twist, burning her wrist. "Damn," she yelled, letting go of the cup and dropping it next to the gear shift where the sticky liquid ran down the side of her light blue dress. "Damn it to hell!"

She stared at the dark brown stain soaking through the thin fabric making the skin on her thigh burn. Quickly she pulled into the lot and eased her Volvo into the first available space.

Ms. Schneider didn't know why the signs always caught her attention. There were a lot of them around here. It certainly wasn't anything new to look at these days. The neighborhood was "in transition," they explained when she got hired. That just meant there were very few white kids going to school here. This high school had once been all white, and so was the neighborhood. But that was a long time ago, before she finished college herself, while answering phones for an insurance company. Her title was "College Counselor." And every day when these kids trailed through her tiny office stacked with papers, she hoped against hope that they just wanted information on how to get into college and didn't tell her that their mother's boyfriend beat up their mother so bad that she ended up in the hospital, had sex with them when nobody could see, were pregnant, or maybe doing speed on the side while they sold drugs. These rare confessions made her face turn red, her throat close, and a cold sweat break out across her body. When they started telling her these things, she felt like she was shrinking, shutting down, disappearing. The image she carried in her head as a wise and highly admired woman dispensing long-waited-for advice to grateful teenagers faded away.

She'd been counseling for a couple of decades now. Her hair had started to gray around her face, showing that the middle years were hurdling toward her faster and faster. There were other changes; her body was heavier, the skin becoming looser, flaccid on the insides of her arms and on her thighs. A fine network of lines branched out around her eyes, and there were deeper lines around her mouth. Her neck sagged, and her back hurt from sitting all day. She'd stopped wearing her "cute heels," in favor of flats because her feet swelled at the ankles and ached most of the day. She wore glasses now. She'd bought a tortoise shell pair with oversize frames. Stylish. They just didn't look as attractive as they did on the twenty-year-old blonde who posed wearing them in the picture predominantly displayed in the window of her optometrist's office.

Ms. Schneider wasn't married. She never really got close. There were a few attempted relationships. They were disappointments. Big ones. Getting dumped hurt. Getting dumped by someone who clearly wasn't worthy of you hurt worse. High expectations were always followed by a big letdown. It was better to face reality and know your limitations. She knew that if you matter to someone, they pay attention to you, They listen when you speak. When you don't matter, they won't care, and you'll end up with regret. The saddest thing was to find out that someone who mattered so much to you, didn't feel you mattered at all to them.

There were less and less opportunities for relationships the older she got. Finally, there weren't any at all. Nobody was looking to romance a middle-aged, (soon to be older than middle-aged) woman. She bought a condo in a nice area with older white neighbors and spent her free time when she wasn't teaching, taking care of her elderly mother who lived in her second bedroom and her two cats, whose toys, dishes and beds consumed the living room. She microwaved all the meals for her mother and herself, and watched television until ten o'clock, when she promptly fell asleep. On Sundays, she took her mother to church. When she felt a little lonely, she read a romance novel and imagined herself as the heroine. Sometimes the sameness of it, the boredom, crept in slowly, suffocating her. She told herself she was lucky. She had more than a lot of people because she'd always played by the rules. If you played by the rules the Lord would see to the rest.

It was easier to teach when she first started. The students still followed rules. They didn't expect her to find them a college placement after they'd dropped any class that required homework, weren't sure where the library was, and passed the classes they were forced to take with courtesy "D's." Those were the days when the student parking lot was stocked with late model sedans that parents owned and let their teenage kids borrow with permission, and the girls wore skin tight designer jeans, big hair, and spike heels. The boys were just as flashy trying to look like rock stars, flinging their carefully styled hair off their face when they talked to you.

Now there were less cars parked in the lot, but they were expensive; Jeeps, flashy sports cars, brightly painted bulky trucks trimmed with chrome that were never used for hauling. It seemed they belonged to the kids themselves these days. The uniform for girls was armfuls of bangles, short skirts, riding high on thin thighs, tiny tops that didn't meet the waist, shredded jeans, baggy army jackets trimmed with decals and embroidery, costing hundreds of dollars, and designer tennis shoes. The boys tucked long greasy hair behind their ears or tied it behind their neck or in a bun on top of their head, if they didn't shave their heads entirely. They favored tennis shoes that cost at least in the triple digits, or heavy military-style boots or sandals that they clutched between their toes, and ripped jeans that sagged to show their boxers.

Everything cost so much money now. The clothes, the cell phones, the cars. She wondered how most of the students afforded it. They didn't all sell drugs. Did they? The neighborhood surrounding the school was congested with block after block of cheap apartments. The kind where people regularly moved in and out. The cars parked in front were older too, she thought. It would be awful to be one of the poorer kids, she thought. The pressure…She'd been poor growing up, but then there weren't so many material things you were expected to have. She'd read somewhere that you couldn't tell class by the way people dressed in the United States. It was the best dressed nation of poor people.

Ms. Schneider turned off the engine, examined her skirt again, sighed, and lowered her head to light a cigarette. She kept it lowered while she inhaled a few times. That was better. The administrators frowned on smoking. Maybe they didn't know that most of the students smoked…..marijuana, and probably other things. Or maybe they didn't want to know.

This semester she'd volunteered to teach basic math in first period. Nothing complicated. Math wasn't her favorite subject, and she hadn't excelled at it the way she did in every other subject when she was in school. They needed someone to run the class until they replaced Mr. Kee, who ate spicy Korean food that left the staff break room smelling of garlic. He'd had a heart attack almost two months ago. Scared the hell out of everyone when he suddenly keeled over and hit the floor while he was pouring coffee and complaining about a young men in his class who pulled his eyes into a slant and began laughing whenever Mr. Kee's name was mentioned. They weren't sure when, or if, Mr. Kee was coming back to work. He carried a full class roster of kids who were not college bound. Ms. Schneider knew he hated his class. She'd watched him grading papers, his face breaking into a wide grin of enjoyment as he slashed through the scribbled calculations with a red pen and wrote large "F's" across the top of the papers.

She thought teaching math might be refreshing, a break from her usual round of programming the kids who could hack it to community college, some with a little more ambition, to state. She was wrong. She shouldn't have been surprised to find that most of the kids who weren't on the college track could barely add. They'd never memorized their times tables. Long division and fractions were a mystery, A lot of them weren't even familiar with the calculator on their cell phones. When one of the students offered to come to the front of the class and demonstrate how to use the calculator on the cell phone, she was relieved, until he explained proudly that he used it to add up the money he made selling weed and subtract what he paid for the stuff initially. *A true entrepreneur*. She didn't call on him again, but that was unnecessary. She heard he was in juvenile hall for burglary. She abandoned the idea of giving any real instruction and checked off the days until Mr. Kee returned.

Ms. Schneider sighed again, still sleepy, and rubbed her wrist that had started to ache. The coffee was wasted, most of it sticking to her skirt. She looked across at the concrete-block wall bordering the parking lot. No matter how many times they painted over it the graffiti artists always triumphed, coming back some time in the night to replace what had been erased. For the last couple of weeks, the "White Power Coalition," and "New White Brotherhood," had been replaced by large black spidery letters that said, "Whites Are Always Your Enemy," and "Rid The World of Whitey Now." She shivered when she looked at the writing. Just across from her classroom was a poster on the window of a boarded-up storefront, only partly scribbled over, that showed the silhouettes of black men pointing machine guns at a family of stick figures painted white (some of the stick figures in the white family were small enough to represent children). Under the silhouettes tall black letters spelled out, "Black Pride Means Knowing Your Enemy." "Eliminate Your Enemy and Save Our Race." "Fuck The Police," and "Revenge George Floyd's Death." The principal had announced over the loudspeaker that the police department was offering a reward for information on the party or parties that kept posting in that place. So far nobody had come forward. Every time she saw the writings she tried to look away, knowing that they were referring to her. She was the enemy. Images of lynched bodies hanging, swaying in the wind. *Their ghosts coming back for revenge.*

Ms. Schneider's first period was free today. A study hall had been assigned to all the students, and in place of her usual class she had counseling sessions scheduled for those who requested them. She stopped by the office on the way to her room and checked her posted list. There was only one name, Adelina Heron. She struggled to place it. A vague image of a large mixed-race girl came to mind. She wasn't sure. The Adelina she remembered was a loudmouth. She didn't look forward to the meeting. What could this girl possibly want? She wasn't one of the students on the college-track. Those were usually the only ones that came to her for help in planning a curriculum that would lead them to college. She decided to get the meeting over quickly before second period, so she could head down the street and get some real coffee, not the generic crap they made in the teacher's breakroom.

After arranging her desk, Ms. Schneider, pulled out Adelina Heron's school file. She was a transfer from another inner-city school, one that was considerably worse than the one where Ms. Schneider worked. This one was a low achiever, a poor reader, who'd been offered tutoring, but never took it. Her aptitude tests were below average. She was also a behavior problem, having two recent suspensions under her belt. One was for threatening a teacher. Ms. Schneider remembered her now, a skulking presence. A tall, overweight girl who stooped to hide her height. She was loud. Always angry. Ms. Schneider heard her yelling in the halls to other kids, "Motherfucker, you get your ass over here!"

She shivered, feeling uncomfortable, exposed in the little cubicle of an office that was located at the end of the corridor where your footsteps stopped echoing. The other offices were empty at this time she remembered. She was the only one scheduled for sessions.

She hesitated when footsteps approached her desk, and kept staring down at her stack of folders, shuffling, and reshuffling a pile of papers to avoid looking up. She could feel the girl's eyes boring through her. Judging, hating.

"I got an appointment now."

Ms. Schneider looked up. The girl was, as she'd feared, the one she'd thought. Adelina was tall, and large-framed. Her shoulders were broad, her arms heavy with padded flesh, and her legs were thick. Trunk-like. She wore a tee shirt that had once been white but now faded to a dirty gray. "Always Remember," was written in large black letters on the front. Below there was a list of names. She recognized them, all Black men and women killed by police in the past year.

It was all over the news. Adelina was large-breasted, and it looked as if she wasn't wearing a bra.

Her breasts sagged and hung askew on her wide chest giving her a matronly air. *Aunt Jemimah?* The nipples were dark against the white of the shirt. Ms. Schneider looked down. Adelina wore a too-short skirt that hiked up in front over her protruding stomach and showed off her wide jiggly thighs. *She shouldn't weigh so much at her age. She's even breathing like she just ran a mile.* Ms. Schneider pictured the girl eating a large order of greasy fries. She struggled to keep her own weight down. Yogurt and vegetables. Pre-packaged low calorie microwave dinners. No red meat and just a few carbs, but it was getting harder every year. *But I refuse to end up like...It just takes discipline, and that's one thing I am about.*

Ms. Schneider gestured toward the single chair in front of her desk. Adelina had tattoos on her arms, devil faces and roses, and a name that Ms. Schneider could not read. Her skin was rough, medium dark and blotchy, Ms. Schneider noted. Acne-scarred in places and covered with a too light foundation that called attention to the pitted skin. Ms. Schneider couldn't read Adelina's eyes. They were outlined heavily in black and hidden behind a double set of false black eyelashes that didn't conceal their lightness and glitter. She wore some kind of a burgundy weave that was secured high on the crown of her head and fell below her shoulders, past her natural black hair. The shiny strands like nylon thread unwound from a spool moved stiffly when Adelina shifted her head. The room seemed suddenly crowded as Adelina sat down in front of her, breathing heavily, occupying the small space.

She spoke first," I'm Ms. Schneider. I'm the college-planning counselor. What can I help you with?" Ms. Schneider forced her lips apart in a smile. She wondered about the girl's race. Some kind of Central American? African American? Not any one in particular, a mixture then? Maybe part Mexican? Was she illegal? She thought about a documentary she'd seen on public television about the Haitian cane workers, how they were treated like slaves, slept on the floor, and were only fed after they picked the first load of cane in the day. *Was that an old documentary? Did they still treat them that way?* She felt her cheeks flush. Most likely, Adelina wasn't Haitian. Anyway, it wasn't Ms. Schneider's fault they treated people that way.

"So, what can I help you with?" Ms. Schneider asked again when she didn't get an answer. She forced herself to look toward the girl's eyes, slits of light amber color peeking out from beneath the black fringe. "I don't see that you've selected a tract program. Did you plan to continue your education once you graduate?" She choked out the word," graduate." Her throat closed. Adelina certainly was not headed to college. Not with that record. She hadn't even finished the basic requirements that she would need to graduate.

"Yeah I'm goin. To college. I'm goin."

Ms. Schneider nodded her head slowly trying to think of what to say. She stared at the girl's tee shirt and her eyes wandered toward the window facing the street, stopping on the sign that showed a Black man pointing a gun. She could feel her heart begin to beat faster. "I see you've had trouble with math. You were assigned a tutor, but I don't see any follow up."

"Nah"

"So, you didn't see the tutor?"

The girl shrugged and looked down at her hands. They were large. The fingers were long and thick, and the palms were a startling white when she opened her hands to unclasp her backpack and set it on the floor. Ms. Schneider noticed her nails, painted a glistening black, except for the index fingers, where the nails were painted a pale yellow and peppered with small rhinestones.

"You need to complete these courses with a "C," or better if you want to go to college. Even community college.

Adelina looked away, her face blank, and didn't answer.

"I could make you a list of classes that you should be taking now. Do you want me to do that?'

"How many times can I take the classes?"

"How many times? What do you mean?"

"I mean when I fail...How many times can I take it again?"

"Well, you shouldn't go in with the idea that you're going to fail. But if you don't complete a class, you can take it again or in night school. Some of the classes are even available in community college."

"So, I can take it again?"

"Yes, of course." Ms. Schneider looked at the test scores in the girls' file and sighed. "Maybe I should find you a reading tutor also."

Adelina stood up suddenly, shoving her chair away. She was suddenly enraged, spitting her words at Ms. Schneider. "I don't need no damn tutor. I don't want nobody knowing I can't read. Knowing I'm stupid!"

Ms. Schneider backed up in her seat. "Just because you have problems with some of the subjects doesn't mean you're stupid. You just may need a little extra help. I can refer you to some place for that." *It wasn't her fault she was so poorly educated.*

Adelina eyed her warily. Her full lips were pursed, covered in a sticky red gloss. Ms. Schneider wondered again what ethnicity Adelina was. She could be anything at all, or several anything's. But she could never be white. Whatever Adelina was, Ms. Schneider knew she'd have to be twice as good at what she knew, and what she did, to get by in this world. That's why everyone knew about the exceptions; the "special ones," the talented ones," the kids called them "Ghetto Fabulous." They were the athletes like Le Braun James, the talented entertainers with gorgeous faces and bodies, like Beyonce, politicians, with exceptional IQ's, east coast law graduates, like President Obama. But they were the extraordinary ones. What happened to people like Adelina who were just average, or maybe below average? The ones who had no particular talent or ability, or if like this girl, weren't even pretty. What kind of life would they live? No point in them even dreaming. They were too far behind to catch up and then become exceptional. They weren't allowed to be mediocre.

Ms. Schneider always counseled by rote. Her voice was soothing and maternal. She used the scripts she'd perfected over the years with hundreds of students. She didn't want to make any waves. Not so close to her retirement on a full pension. She encouraged the student's dreams when she could, praised them for their goals, and their future plans. Suggested avenues that were in reach, assured them they could do anything they set their mind to, as long as it was reasonable.

She wondered about Adelina's history. A broken home no doubt. Foster care. Homelessness. Molestation and drugs. They all were cast from the same mold, destined to come to a bad end one way or another. At the end of a police bullet or a drug overdose. Her life would always be shifting and unreliable. *She'll be promiscuous and have lots of kids. She'll support them with welfare. She will outlive us all.*

"So, you're doing alright in your classes. Aren't you?" She knew the answer to that but couldn't think of anything else to say. *Why was this girl here anyway?* She forced herself to look up at Adelina who was standing over her desk, glaring. Adelina, looking hostile and threatening. Ms. Schneider felt a cold chill run down her body and her face flushing. Adelina was so tall and looked so strong, The muscles in her arms stretched under her skin like knotted rope. You could see she was angry, and the way she stood with her hands on her hips was insolent, disrespectful. At any moment she could become unhinged and do…something. Ms. Schneider bit her lip, wishing she hadn't said anything to upset her. Adelina was moving closer to the desk. Her eyes were narrowed. What if she pulled out a weapon? Ms. Schneider pushed her chair further back and huddled in her seat. She would scream if the girl came closer. Somebody had to hear. Her hands were shaking. She grabbed a pen in her right hand, relieved as she felt her palm close over the plastic cylinder. She would stab Adelina if she had to. Right in the neck where the main arteries were.

"I just…" Adelina looked down at the floor, backing up as she spoke and set the chair back closer to the desk. Her voice was quieter now.

Ms. Schneider felt her body go limp and cold sweat begin to collect at her hairline. She waited.

"Just in case…I wanted to know. Maybe I'll take those classes sometime."

"Those classes?" Ms. Schneider was puzzled. "Which ones?"

"The classes you take to go to college. Like you said."

"Oh." Ms. Schneider looked down at the Student Profile and all of the Achievement Test Scores recorded on the face sheet.

Adelina had not passed her High School Exit Exam. "You know, sometimes it's not the best idea. I mean, college is not for everybody. Especially if you don't have…" She stopped herself. "Sometimes people don't have it up here." She tapped her forehead lightly.

Adelina stared at her unblinkingly.

"You need a lot to get ahead in this world, especially if you want to go to college. You need the smarts. Something going for you. Otherwise, it will never work." Ms. Schneider felt a deepening sadness. It wasn't fair. She couldn't be part of this sham. She couldn't help Adelina delude herself, subject herself to scorn, derision, and pity.

Outside the window by the chain link fencing a few feral cats played in the grass. The custodian put poison out to kill them, but they were too smart to eat the pellets, hungry and skinny as they were, ribs floating to the surface of their scabby backs. An orange cat with a torn ear limped over and began rolling in the grass, momentarily enjoying the sunlight, his eyes partially closed, oozing liquid. Ms. Schneider wondered how these cats survived. She knew some of the teachers fed them scraps. But why? Why prolong their miserable life?

She turned back to Adelina. "So, your question was?"

"Just if I could take those classes again?"

"Was that it?"

Adelina shrugged. "Guess so."

Ms. Schneider felt foolish. Was Adelina trying to tell her that she thought she'd been born for more than what she could achieve? "You know sometimes with a particular student, it's not that important if they finish high school. If they plan to go out and work for instance."

Adelina leaned forward, mentioning "work," had caught the girl's attention. Ms. Schneider could see her breasts straining against her too-tight low-cut blouse. Ms. Schneider looked away.

“Finishing the year here won’t really make a difference in your plans if you are going to work anyway. “Do you think you’re learning anything now?”

Adelina lost interest as soon as that question was asked and looked at Ms. Schneider blankly.

“Don’t know.”

“Well, if you’re not really learning anything, maybe you’re just wasting your time when you could be earning money. Probably helping your family out. And you’re taking up space from a student that really wants to learn and has an academic future. Doesn’t that make sense?”

Adelina’s eyes followed the pen Ms. Schneider gripped in her hand. Ms. Schneider hastily dropped it.

“I have job referrals you know. Sometimes we get them in. We used to post them in the hall, but they took down the bulletin board when they painted and never put it back.” Still keeping a cautious eye on Adelina, she reached into her desk and pulled out a notebook.

“Here’s one. Burlington Cleaners needs a counterperson, from three until seven thirty, Monday through Saturday. What do you think?”

Adelina stood up very slowly, peeling her puckered thighs away from the wooden chair where they’d gotten stuck in the damp air that settled in the small office. Her voice was louder now. Harsh. “No. It’s too dirty. My mama worked in one. Hot as hell. Pressing clothes all day.”

“No, that’s not it,” Ms. Schneider said. “You would be working at the counter, giving people their orders, taking orders.”

“No.” Adelina’s voice grew louder. More resolute.

“Well, there’s another one. Actually, if you weren’t enrolled any longer in school, you could work there full time. It’s a factory downtown. They make clothes…women’s clothes. You know, like you buy in the stores. They’ll teach you how to operate a sewing machine. That’s a skill all young ladies should have.”

"A sewing factory?" Adelina asked.

"Well, yes. If you learned to sew…who knows? Maybe you could even design clothes or something like that." She finished lamely, her voice trailing off. *Making things you can't afford to own.*

"I failed sewing." Adelina informed her. "I hate it." She looked down at her feet, embarrassed, remembering working on one gym bag all semester, sewing and ripping out her work whenever she made it to class. Her teacher was never satisfied with what she'd done. She watched as her classmates completed other projects, skirts, blouses, a few even got as far as dresses. "Fuck sewing."

"Well, I guess that's all I have right now. But once you aren't coming here, you'll have much more time to look for work."

"Not coming here?"

"Aren't you…Didn't you say that you weren't going to finish school?"

"No, you said I wasn't."

"I was just… I don't want you to get in over your head. Try for more than you're capable." Ms. Schneider thought about the few top students she recommended to four-year universities. How proud she was when they were accepted. It was a feather in her cap too.

"I've gotta leave." Adelina stood up quickly, shoving her chair to the side, and tossing her backpack over her shoulder.

"Have we resolved anything? I mean what are your plans?" Ms. Schneider noticed that Adelina seemed to be looking at her hair. She pushed her no-color hair that needed washing behind her ears, then followed the girl's eyes more closely. Adelina was staring at Ms. Schneider's certificates and licenses that hung on the wall behind her desk. Adelina's eyes moved down the row of frames from left to right, and then turned and walked out without looking back. Ms. Schneider felt that she should say something to the girl, but she wasn't sure what.

For the next few days, she didn't see Adelina around the campus. After a few more days, Ms. Schneider checked Adelina's homeroom where attendance was taken and saw that Adelina hadn't come to school. At the end of the week, her name still was showing up as absent in the attendance report. After another week passed, it seemed that Adelina had simply vanished. The only recent record of her was Ms. Schneider's note in her student file on their meeting. The column for "Counseling Action Taken," was blank because she hadn't made any entries in the Individual Education Plan.

For the next few weeks, Ms. Schneider felt distracted, uneasy, even when she was dealing with the college prep students, the easy ones. The ones who everybody thought made counseling so gratifying. On Saturday morning she drove over to the housing project which was the last address Adelina had provided. She checked the mailboxes and located the name, "Heron." With some trepidation, she climbed the cracked staircase with a partially missing rail to the second floor and knocked on apartment 204. There was no answer. The blinds were pulled up, and she peered inside. The apartment appeared empty. The only furniture remaining was a fold-up cot in the front room. After she knocked a few more times she gave up and went downstairs.

Ms. Schneider checked with the manager in the first apartment. The manager answered the door on her fourth knock. She was an older woman with steel-gray hair, crunched tight, still in her threadbare, cotton housecoat and worn, fuzzy black slippers planted at the end of her skinny bowed legs. *They look like bison hooves from the taxidermy display at the museum,* Ms. Schneider thought. *Why isn't she dressed? It's almost noon.* "Does the Heron family still live here?"

The woman regarded her suspiciously, hands on her hips. Nobody but cops or social workers ever inquired about the tenants. "Who's asking?

Ms. Schneider explained who she was and that she was looking for a student.

After studying her, the manager answered, "They moved out a month or so ago."

Ms. Schneider walked back to her car. The family had moved from here before Adelina ever came to see her. She checked again at school on Monday, but there was no transfer address.

So, Adelina was gone. Most likely Ms. Schneider would never see her again, but the image of the girl standing over her desk remained. Menacing, angry about their meeting. Adelina was now the one holding the pen, ready to stab her with it. But that's not really what happened, she told herself. Anyway, what was I supposed to say to her? We only have a small handful of students that make it to college from here. She wasn't going to be one of them. But the figure kept reappearing in her thoughts. Sometimes Ms. Schneider pictured Adelina elsewhere, the images crawled across her eyes; a prostitute strolling down the Boulevard approaching slowing cars, or maybe in one of the orange jumpsuits that the inmates wore in the county jail, staring out behind bars, or worse, the khaki uniform worn by the women in prison up north in Dublin California.

When the images began their race through her head she told herself that it wasn't her problem.

Adelina's life was destined before she ever came into the picture.

Sometimes late at night stumbling half asleep to the kitchen for a drink of water, she saw a crooked shadow in the entryway, fleeing across the hall. The shadow was large, looming. It waited by the bedroom door so that she had to run past it as fast as she could to go back to bed. There she would lie with her heart pounding and the covers pulled up to her chin. Some nights she heard noises, a deep raspy, wheezing sound like trapped breath accompanied by a low droning murmur that seemed to be coming closer and closer to her bed. *She's here!* Ms. Schneider would close her eyes and pray for the sound to stop. On the mornings after she would find her mother asleep and snoring in the living room where she'd wandered from her bed.

As ten more years passed, Ms. Schneider found herself looking at an old woman in the mirror, a depressed old woman, who trudged off to her counseling job at the high school joylessly every day. Her mother became more of a problem. She was eighty now, and Ms. Schneider began to think she would have to retire from counseling a little earlier than she'd anticipated. It was becoming harder to leave her mother alone all day. Her mother would start to boil something on the stove and leave the gas burner on until the pan caught fire. Several times she filled the bathtub and let it run over onto the floor, and into the hall. The carpet mildewed and had to be replaced. Ms. Schneider was informed that she was responsible. Twice last week her mother wandered off by herself during the day and got lost. The last time, police ended up bringing her back after finding her sitting alone at a bus stop in the pouring rain. The only reason they knew where she lived was because she was carrying an envelope addressed to Ms. Schneider that she'd taken from the kitchen table. Ms. Schneider hired a caregiver to spend the days with her mother, but after her third day there, Ms. Schneider's mother complained that she didn't like the woman. On the fourth day she locked the caretaker out of the house and Ms. Schneider had to leave school to let the caretaker back inside so she could get her purse and quit.

After some thought, Ms. Schneider decided to place her mother in assisted living. After checking out the various ones available, she learned that there was a program that provided financial assistance to families to help pay for a decent placement for an elderly relative. *A kind of welfare*, she said to herself, amused. Ms. Schneider never thought she would be applying for financial help through a government program…but here she was.

No matter what they said, teachers and school personnel never made enough money.

She took the day off work when she was scheduled to meet with the county social worker, the individual who would screen her to see if she qualified for financial aid combined with her mother's social security to enroll her mother in assisted living. Ms. Schneider was nervous, worrying about leaving her mother alone, so nervous that she'd locked the apartment door from the outside twice this week, and then chewed her nails all day, worried in case there was a fire, and her mother was trapped inside.

She waited along with others in the public welfare office, careful to sit as far away as possible from the rest of the people. *You could never tell what you might catch in a place like this.* There were no magazines to read and the people waiting stared up at a large television screen. A talk show was playing, and the guests sitting around a circular table were laughing. The subject was "how to spot your spouse cheating." The studio audience was invigorated. They all had some bit of personal information they wanted to share on television. Ms. Schneider's face flushed red as she listened. She was so grateful she'd followed her instincts, played it safe, and never got herself into a situation like the ones described. A young woman sitting a few chairs down with three small children seated on the dirty tile floor at her feet, shook her fist, and yelled at the screen, "You kick his two-timing ass to the curb!"

Ms. Schneider turned away from the sound, and watched out of the corner of her eye, as the youngest child sitting next to the woman grew bored and tired and stretched out on the gray, sticky floor. His mother, engrossed in the program she was watching, did not seem to notice.

"Ms. Agnes Schneider?"

She jerked upright. Something familiar in that voice she recognized. *What was it?*

"I'm calling Ms. Agnes Schneider."

Ms. Schneider looked up at the tall, large-bodied woman standing a few feet away, one hand on her hip. She was probably in her early or mid-thirties, had a medium brown complexion, carefully made up, and precisely styled hair, tucked under at the ends. She wore a tasteful navy business suit, and tall high heels that added to her height and gave her an air of imposition. As she stepped closer, Ms. Schneider could see she was somewhat heavy in the hips and legs, and her bust strained the seams of her plain white blouse visible through her open jacket. Ms.

Schneider looked at the woman's face. *Where did she know it from?*

"You're Ms. Schneider? Come with me please."

She followed the woman through the open door and down the hall to a small government office with a metal desk, filing cabinet, and two folding chairs.

"Please sit down," The woman gestured toward one of the chairs facing her desk. The phone rang, and she raised one finger to pause, and answered it.

Ms. Schneider studied the woman's eyes. There was something recognizable in their glitter, outlined carefully in heavy black liner. Something from an awfully long time ago. The woman spoke briefly in Spanish, and then put down the phone.

"I'm Ms. Carson, I'm the geriatric social worker," she introduced herself. "I need to evaluate your financial situation and based on my determination you will either be awarded one of our Care Grants for the families of seniors, or I'll let you know that you don't qualify."

"Ms. Carson?" Ms. Schneider could feel her heart pounding, her throat closing. She stared at the woman's long, thick fingers stretched across her keyboard. The nails were short and rounded, polished a soft pastel pink to match her lipstick. "Do you have another name? I mean a maiden name?" *Was that the word for it?* She felt herself blush. "I mean…I thought I knew you when I saw you."

"Ms. Carson is my name. I don't think we've met." The words were crisp, enunciated clearly. Ms. Carson began typing on her computer and did not look back at Ms. Schneider. "Let's get started here. I'm going to ask you a series of questions to see if you qualify for our aid package."

Ms. Schneider studied the carefully made-up face; coarse, somewhat thick skin, pitted here and there with acne scars, covered with concealer, a little too light for the woman's complexion. Ms. Schneider felt a cold chill run down her back as she answered the questions. She could feel the woman watching her, judging, even though her eyes were focused on the computer screen. "I'm sure I know you.." Ms. Schneider started again.

Ms. Carson raised an eyebrow. "Well, I can't think of where."

Was she wrong? Did Ms. Schneider hear what sounded like disdain in the woman's voice? Her face began to burn. *How dare she judge*! But she could judge, Ms. Schneider knew that! That's exactly what she was here to do. She kept her eyes on the floor as she answered Ms. Carson's questions. *Does she recognize me too?*

"Well," Ms. Carson squinted at the screen, "Based on the figures you've given me, it appears that you do have enough disposable income to contribute for your mother's placement without a county subsidy. I'm going to send your file up for final review, and you'll receive a written letter notifying you of the county's decision."

"It seems you've made up your mind," Ms. Schneider choked. *This woman had the power to make a decision that would change her whole life*. The only way she would be able to contribute to her mother's assisted living placement would be if she kept working until she, herself, was in her eighties, if that was possible, and if she moved to a tiny single apartment in the low-rent part of town to save as much as possible on rent. Even then it probably wouldn't be enough. She was sure her mother would live to be one hundred, maybe older. By her own admission, she was strong as an ox. "It's just a school counselor's salary after all," she mumbled, looking down, focusing on Ms. Carson's desk.

Ms. Carson heard Ms. Schneider's voice and stared back at her across the desk, frowning. She was leaning back in her chair, holding a pen in her right hand, clicking it on and off. Fear raced through Ms. Schneider's body, making her heart suddenly start to pound. She remembered holding a pen just that way so many years ago. Then she'd thought of it as a weapon. *What was Ms. Carson thinking? Did she want revenge?*

"You can always appeal our denial. The instructions for appeal will be in the envelope with the decision. A school counselor's salary is quite substantial," she added, by way of justification. "I see people all day who earn only minimum wage. Those people are in desperate need of county subsidies." Her voice chastised, directing Ms. Schneider to see how fortunate she was.

Ms. Schneider had to know. "Did you go to Webster High School about fifteen years or so ago?"

Ms. Carson smiled. "No, I don't believe so. I went to several schools, but not there. Are you feeling ill? You are as pale as a ghost."

"I remember you!" Ms. Schneider heard herself shout. 'I'm sure it was you."

"Really?" Ms. Carson smiled slightly and raised her eyebrow. "You're mistaking me for someone else."

"No!" Ms. Schneider felt a shudder pass through her body remembering the fear she'd felt. You didn't forget something like that. *How could that same person now be in charge of making a decision that would affect Ms. Schneider's life forever?* She stared at Ms. Carson, who'd risen and was now standing at the doorway, her large frame filling the space, the same way Ms. Schneider remembered her inside her own office space so long ago. *But could it really be her? How had she gotten to this place?* Ms. Schneider would not have been at all surprised to find out Adelina was dead, homeless, or living on the street. Just not this. Not here! "What's your first name, if you don't mind me asking?" she heard her voice, pleading.

"I don't mind at all. My first name's Roberta. Does that solve it for you? Now if you don't mind me asking, should I call someone for you? You still look like you're going to faint."

Ms. Schneider shook her head and stumbled out to the building lobby, and then into the hazy, smoggy Los Angeles sunlight, where she sat down on a bench in front of the building and breathed in the noxious black fumes from the passing busses. Her eyes burned and watered. *I've seen too much, that's why my eyes are so tired.* She pictured Adelina again, with her slovenly clothes, garish make up and fingernails, and her way of looking away and answering in monosyllables when she spoke. No, this is a different person. No similarity here.

For no reason at all, she turned and looked back toward the building. The sun had shifted, and late afternoon light flooded the building lobby. She could see directly across the tiled floor. Ms. Schneider thought she saw Adelina standing in the doorway looking out at her. She hurried toward the building. *She had one last chance. She would tell this Ms. Carson she knew who she really was and find out why she was using a different name.* But when she pushed open the heavy glass door, the lobby was empty. She thought she could hear the "tap, tap," of women's high heels moving rapidly down the corridor.

Stagnation

Rachid Toumi

The sun was blazing outside. The marine gusts coming across the Canary Islands and up the sloping hill squeezed through the ajar pigeon hole-like window and cooled our faces and feet as we sat silent on sheepskin in the room that was shaped like a piece of triangular cheese and that faced the big blue sea. We got ourselves comfortably seated opposite each other to avoid the nakedness of being watched from behind: My father was formed in the military, Chapar, my childhood pal, came from the underworld of *La Gare*. I mirrored their behavior because I came to realize—too late—that their self-preservation exceeded what little love had remained in their hardened hearts. I leaned back against the peeling blue-and-white painted wall, the aroma of the seaweed-smelling breeze feeling sweet in my nostrils, and cast one last look at my alter egos. This would not be my last summer in this savage Saharan strip of the Atlantic but I knew that that time was fast approaching and I had to begin with the writing.

It seemed that the pleasantly drowse-inducing effect of the oceanic breeze was not enough a tranquilizer for my old man who now stealthily and swiftly swallowed two pills of Xanax, lay quietly down, and slowly closed his eyes. In a minute or so, he crossed the border and the *Giardia Fronteriza* at the north-western part of Ifni shot at him. When they discovered he was only a child, they ceased shooting, as he disappeared among the Argan trees. It was sunset and he lay against the slanting broad trunk of the biggest spinosa in the center of the wood and slept, exhausted from walking the whole day on an empty stomach, tracking down his cow.

At dawn, he heard its faint mooing. He sprang to his feet and ran toward open terrain, as his loved one emerged swaggering out of the Argan bush. The kid watched her milk-dripping breasts with contentment and I watched how the tense muscles of the man's face repose; it was more the effect of the chemical antidote than it was that of the happy denouement of a child's anecdote. He had told me that this childhood memory was of late recurrently relived in his mind and that the overdose of the strong medical drug helped him recuperating it in its original form and vivid aliveness. In fact, the tale was well-told and you could not tell what was fact and what was Xanax.

Chapar, red-eyed, looked confused from smoking cannabis in the daytime. He sipped the cold tea and zoomed in on his phone wallpaper. A photo of fading color of the young man standing on a red carpet and holding in his right hand the microphone, face beaming with delight. The screen reflected the shadow of his aging pan, scarred and unnaturally brown. He blinked. The looming reflection dwindled in the background, giving way to the budding projection in the foreground. In an instant, the hashish-driven animation carried him to the light at the entrance of *La Gare* of the nineties of the previous century. The dazzling luminosity blinded him just before it swallowed him up.

La Gare was at the time the brightest place in the city: the circus, gambling-cafés, contraband-stores, telephone-booths, billiard-rooms, snake-charmers, oral story-tellers, herb-sellers, and hashish-dealers. Chapar once caught me unawares, staring at the powder-cheeked and red stick-lipped lean and tall man dressed in a woman's *jellaba*[1]. The figure stood stately and motionless as a statue except for the seducingly half-smiling eyes. I thought the man was a woman. 'That's a faggot,' the older buddy corrected

[1] *A traditional loose garment with sleeves worn by men and women in the Maghreb region.*

me as though he was a schoolteacher instructing his pupil. Crude teaching. No pedagogy. I shook off the shock as I elbowed myself through the crowd, walked past the big square, originally a small-sized stadium, sat at the tribune, and watched. Chapar, tall, dark, and big-eyed, was the star of the whole show: hand-gloved fighting a peer in the ring, riding a bike too small for his body, pushing hard a corroded swing to breaking point—the child it carried screaming—bullying when caught cheating playing cards, hugging and kissing hard a whore standing at a half-open door behind the *tribun*e at the foot of the dried *oued*[1]—she resisting and laughing—begging a hashish-dealer for a *jwan*[2], snatching a pack of cigarettes from the hands of a tobacco street-vendor and running and laughing—the poor devil had to learn the next time to give a cigarette for free or lose the whole pack to the leaping monkey who became a wolf in times of crisis and took refuge in his stronghold down the *oued.*

My old man would find us in the pool hall in *La Gare*, give me ten dirhams, and say in a military tone to Chapar—who had just moved swiftly like a leopard to the far corner of the place upon seeing him coming—'Take care of the kid,' looking him all the while straight in the eyes. He would keep him locked in that mystic eye contact until he made sure the Dokali[3] decoded the signal. He got into the habit of omitting parts of his utterances—in fact the most important ones—for effect, in ways similar to the art of the great masters of short story-telling like Hemingway. The difference was that Papa, unlike my papa, had no way as a writer to look the reader straight in the eye to make sure that understanding took place. Some Hemingway!

They were startled by the abrupt voice of the *moadin*[4]. You could see that in the widening of their blood-shot eyes. 'May Allah curse Satan,' they said, or rather, yawned in a jarring note that was almost beastly roar. Barely two minutes later: 'May Allah for-

---

[1] *A valley in North Africa; usually dry except in the rainy season.*
[2] *A piece of hashish enough to make a cigarette.*
[3] *From Dokala, region in north-west Central Morocco.*
[4] *The person who calls for prayers from the minaret of a mosque (using a loudspeaker).*

give,' simultaneously in a sigh as they folded the prayer mats. *Cocotte-minute*. Plus cannabis and Xanax. But only drinking is forbidden in Islam, and Chapar gave up drinking years ago. Xanax, my old man said, was mere medicine. We had fish for lunch; my elder, still chewing a big morsel with his cigarette-blackened gums, retreated back into his cave-like slumbering place in the narrower interior of the room in which he did most of his overthinking.

Chapar and I cautiously descended the rocky hill as a shortcut to the beach. The sound of the crashing waves overwhelmed our silence as we sat on the pebbly sand in *Casa Baña*, hidden from view behind the high rocks beyond the dilapidated shrine of Sidi Ifni the *wali*[1]. I drank my wine and Chapar smoked his cannabis for quite a while. 'This' more chemistry than hashish; the golden age of *La Gare* had gone forever,' the husky voice erupted like a muffled rumbling thunder through the thick, slowly-moving, undulating white clouds of smoke in the glaring sunlight. The heavy smoke rode the air currents past the splashing white waves and vanished into the blue vastness. Staring at the sea and at the lightly rocking sailing boats, I recalled how happy I was the day Chapar brought me from Agadir a photocopy of *The Old Man and the Sea*. I was still at high school when he went to Agadir to pursue his higher studies at the Department of History at Ibn Zohr University. He gave up smoking hashish and began to develop withdrawal symptoms—terrible headaches and acute forms of distraction. He bumped into the library's glass wall in broad daylight and the glass splintered and flew amidst the stampeding and the terror. 'Mines everywhere,' he said. He had barely spent three months in Agadir, rarely stepping outside the facilities of the dormitory, before he decided to go back south to the terminal in Tan-Tan. 'I hate the bourgeoisie,' he said. His sweeping quasi-philosophical comments did not stop at the gate of *La Gare*. 'The ragtag is predominantly ruled by instinct,' he whispered as he

[1] *Saint*

watched Ifis and Jdi through the windowpane of the bus at the back entrance of the terminal fighting over some trivial thing as usual, the dust rising and lingering above their heads.

Chapar worked as a barber and settled down. He hired two girls to run the adjacent females hair-do and cosmetics salon, and his small business was noticeably thriving. I called on him one morning in his salon but the place was closed and he was nowhere to be seen. I finally found him loitering in *La Gare* penniless. 'That's a pimp's job, brother,' he said, avoiding eye contact. 'The rent was expensive, anyway,' he continued.

Then he was beating his wife afterward, falling back on his old habit of beating prostitutes with his big, rough hands. 'To tame them,' he said. He had spent a thousand and one nights at the infamous brothels of Zankat Tijara[1], often turning the next day with a swollen black eye or a lame leg. He did not leave bed for weeks when vengeful whores had fed him poison in delicious stew on alcoholic nights. 'Those displaced camp-followers can be much more dangerous than a soldier or a *Coreano* fisherman in the quarter. They could've cut *it* out from the root,' he said as he thanked Allah. By some miracle, Chapar, the wild cat that he was, let go of the grip of death and sprung into the jungle again.

I had always marveled at Chapar's incredible immune system. My mother, who used to like him, said it was hereditary. We had listened to the popular Cheikha Hamdaouia on the radio singing about Dokala ("tall and high like a Dokali!") long before we had the chance to watch these tough men from close toiling in the *Souk* or in the port. They were always associated in our minds with physical strength and manual labor. But there is another side to Chapar, tender and sensitive. I felt my skin creeping at rare drinking sessions when he spoke in the soft voice of a woman, Ray music and the memory of a sweetheart forming the background in the dim setting. It was as though his masculine coarse voice was incongruent with the feminine soft melody of love. If

[1] *Literally, "trading neighborhood."*

he was too drunk to stand guard at the edge of his consciousness in such moments of emergency, especially in the presence of men like my father, his unconscious mind had been trained to regulate entrance to his underground changing room.

If Chapar was the master of the art of silence and concealment, my old man's main self-defense strategy consisted in gaslighting. He had just returned from hajj when I last saw him. We were having a walk in *Barandilla* downtown when he suddenly attacked me. Old habits die hard. He would choose the right time and place to launch his assault in a way that guaranteed that you took it as a crucified man would. If you made the slightest effort to let go of his clenching claws, he would raise his voice systematically gradually, studying your eyes as the quick carious glances of passersby were attracted by the mounting tension between father and son.

'Why did you tell everybody I incarcerated your mother? Perhaps you confused me with one of the villains of your captivity stories,' he began his attack. His needle-like eyes were twitching aggressively as they pierced mine. I knew what the looks meant: I was a traitor.

'I was a witness,' I replied.

'I recall nothing of that sort,' he almost shouted.

I remembered at that moment how he made us suffer in the military hospital in Oued Noun when he had feigned paralysis as part of his recent full-scale war on mother, and I hated him. He was a gifted actor and he fooled even the surgeons, let alone the then innocent me. 'That's an archaic pattern,' my mother warned me. I contemplated the tall figure with the untidy white beard jutting out of the grey *jellaba*, and launched my counter-attack when we reached hotel *Suerte Loca*.

'The mosque is just around the corner; let's both swear on the Quran.'

He hesitated, and I knew I got him. He could have still sworn, but he knew I was attacking the integrity of his pilgrimage to the

Holy House of God. If he had sworn, it would have stripped him of his last attached garments: the image of the nudity of his slackened and shrunken privates in such a public trial was unbearable. He was a dangerous calculating overthinker but I was faster because I no longer trusted him. He was finally relieved when my mobile phone rang. I answered the incoming call and it was Chapar saying he was under arrest.

When Chapar slapped his wife with the spade-like palm of his hand in front of her younger brother and kids, she fought back with a knife and reported him to the police and he ended up once again at the police station. I had already warned him. "I have to run; I'll drop by in the evening," was his response. I put a crisp blue banknote in the breast pocket of his jacket. A timid smile, then he left. I used both argument and dough to make my case convincing with both Chapar and father. Money first to make them listen first. But my pedagogy was a fiasco. When Chapar was back that evening he was back in his intellectual terminal again.

'What a woman wants from a man is protection,' my childhood bodyguard said, eyes beaming with pride and spite. I felt stung by Chapar's insinuation and took it out in a story I flung at his glass masculine mask. It was both revenge and warning.

'You know the Egyptian movie titled "Hello America," starring Adel Imam?' I began. The telling of the story came out of the blue and Chapar's eyes grew suspicious. 'It's about this Bikhit and his fiancée, Adila, and how they came to immigrate to the U.S. and settle at the spacious house of his cousin,' I continued. 'The cousin's wife was American and she gave Adila a pistol to use for self-defense. The girl was about to leave the house when Bikhit came across her in the hallway. She was half-naked in her garment and he stared at the nudity. She told him she wanted to do the shopping and he reminded her that a woman, after all, needs a man to *protect* her. She showed him the pistol, and then made toward the door.'

'I have to run,' Chapar interrupted. 'It's almost sunset and the *moadin* is about to call for prayers; barely time for ablution. See you later,' he said.

'Think about *it*,' I shouted as he zigzagged down the narrow and steep stairs of my apartment in Tan-Tan.

And here he was in custody at the police station smelling of sweat and fear and forced to think about *it* behind the closed iron door of the cell with the barred windows. We never spoke afterward about the movie nor about the humiliation of his detention, the same way we feigned that nothing had happened at Zankat Tijara when he showed up the following day with a bruised eyeball or an injured limb. This was the Chapar that I knew since I was a child: He wanted freedom, then power, then peace, and even peace was not forthcoming.

Chapar was an early bird. He hit the road back to Tan-Tan in the early morning; he would be by now playing cards in the café in *La Gare*. I had breakfast with my old man in the garden at the back of the house. He was chewing nervously while looking at the plants. I watched how tiny pieces of bread sprayed out of his toothless mouth, at the corners of which saliva was foaming in minute bubbles. Sometimes mom nagged about the way he ate, including the disgusting burping, and it was always met with rude or violent reactions.

'I had a dream last night. The big tree over yonder was somehow mysteriously uprooted,' he said and gave me half a minute to process the symbol. Then: 'That was your mother.'

I held my head in my right hand.

'Put up with it, son, I have no one to talk to in this world.'

'As the Saharan Bedouins say, the milk had been shaken until it became sour. You are still shaking it!'

'Your mom had never been as recalcitrant; I don't know why.'

'More than too late for such regurgitation. Slave rebellion. You know she had already sued you. The bad news is that the judge had just passed his verdict ruling that the alimony for the divorce the law requires you to pay is two hundred thousand dirhams.'

'What?'

'The New Family Code. Backed by powerful *men* in the system!'

'Betrayal, Betrayal!'

It was farewell time as the summer vacation came to an end. The CTM made its last turn to leave Ifni, and I looked sadly through the windowpane at the hilltop where my father's house was located. The hill was shrouded in early-morning coastal fog and receded back slowly in the opposite direction as the bus gathered momentum. I was divided between nostalgia and relief as the phantom of the forsaken old man was forming in my mind. I let go of my phantom the moment the bus pierced the city gate, and preoccupied my mind scanning the cactus-covered hills on both sides, the road meandering through like a giant snake crawling feverishly fast. I watched the agile goats atop Argan trees and the flocks of chickens cautiously advancing on the fields, big red hens taking the lead, clucking. 'That's language,' the forlorn man said as he fed the chickens in the garden of the house. 'Observe how the rooster clucks gently and motions for the fat chicken to start eating. He wouldn't have *behaved* that way hadn't she submitted to his superior male will,' the illiterate man concluded his laboratorial observation with an authoritative tone of voice the like of which you would rarely come across even among the scientific community. That was once his scientific as well as metonymic response to my naïve reconciliatory effort between him and my mother. I felt nausea and did not know whether it was the mountainous road or the repulsive theory that caused the sensation.

Father and Chapar, who worked once as *bricoleurs*, were very bad even at *bricolage*. They still wanted to get some money out of it, squeezed out of my generous pocket. Look at the imprints of their crude and clumsy hands all over my flat. Look at the walls and what Chapar did to them with that damn yellowish paint. How ugly my bedroom window looked with that rusty serpentine iron wire hammered to serve as a curtain rod.

'Father, I don't like it.'

'Son, nobody would see it.'

'My girl would,' my lips moved lightly without forming the words. I said instead: '*I* would; how about the aesthetic side and its effect on my temper?'

He grumbled and went about his *bricolage*. They said they would fix everything. How grotesque! And now they made a point of wanting to be intellectual. They presented themselves as preachers of the *natural theory* got from the natural world and vindicated by personal experience. 'Look at the animals!' They would say. The great *bricoleurs*!

I was still in a state of hangover and my head swung with the swinging vehicle.

The uprooted tree. A phallic symbol upside down. Perhaps. Why didn't he circumcise us until we were in primary school, our thing sprouting like that? What a shame! Without an anesthetic. Six nurses to hold each boy firm in that Jahannam. Was it simply carelessness? To engrave with fire in the depth of our being what it means to be a man, the thing being the most valuable thing a man possesses? That was the time children begin to remember things. Not without trauma. To hell with your bricolage!

Jabar /jəba:r/ means the Almighty. How about the name, "Chapar" /tʃeipər/? Not to his face. He might take the diminutive as an insult. 'At La Gare you have to make sure your belt is fastened tight. 'Teacher, you would understand women better the day you could no longer have an erection.' Some Chapar!

'Son, on their wedding night, she gave him a hard kick in the stomach. She ran away in that direction and the whole household were running after her until they caught her and brought her back to the bedroom. She was a wild girl and they had to hold her firm

for him as she screamed and struggled to release herself from their firm grip.'

'Father, wasn't that bestial as well as traumatic?'

'No, it was natural. The next morning she was doing the laundry and singing!'

'And why is he now an abandoned sickly old man stinking at the corner of that filthy room here in this obscure neighborhood?'

'Not his fault. It was the male children to blame. Like it or not, the future relationship between husband and wife necessarily has its basis in that first night. Look at the animals! But of course, variations develop from generation to generation. I've never treated your mother the way I had seen my father treat my mother.'

'Father, be careful. The relationship between child and mother is uterine.'

'What's that?'

'I mean, instinctual; we can't do anything about it. You are alienating your offspring that way.'

'I can't do anything about it, either, son. I wept at your grandfather's grave, but felt nothing at your grandmother's. What time is it? Let us have our lunch. You look like a plucked hen. How can you marry that way!'

The bus came to a stop. 'Tan-Tan, Tan-Tan, Tan-Tan,' came the throaty voice of the driver. For a second, I thought the voice was Chapar's. I had supper with my mother in Zankat Reguibat, and walked to my apartment a few blocks away. I turned on the lamp on the night table, then the radio. A Spanish voice erupted and with it my heart contracted. *Ambush. I'd better keep the phantom locked.* I switched off the transistor, had a double shot of Ballantine, then a shower. I washed my face in the sink with cold water and dried it with a white towel, all the while resisting looking at the damn mirror. I gave up. Emaciated face, bad teeth. Wrinkles, already. The once big eyes were promising to be a chicken's. *It's his face.* I felt utter repulsion. *My mind is traumatized and it will get me there.* I went back to the bedroom, lay down, and closed my eyes. I stood at the edge of the gigantic cliff and hesitated. *They are at your back. Don't turn back. You'd better get going before they get you. Jump forward!* And I jumped into the void and vast darkness. When I opened my eyes, I was at Robinson Crusoe's island.

Interview With a Cathedral

Mike Ross

"I'm not really a cathedral," she sniffs in Catalonian, the native language here in Barcelona, Spain. She shrugs a little for emphasis. "I'm just a church with a fancy name, La Sagrada Familia. You can call me Sagra if you want." Her attention is drawn to a swirl of motion on the main floor. She turns back to me. "Just a moment, please. I have to attend to something."

She turns her focus to a young family who has just entered. A priest approaches them and guides them to a side altar. The young woman holds a tiny infant and the scene glows like a Michelangelo painting, mother and infant, father hovering nearby. The priest mutters a prayer in Spanish, pours a bit of water on the baby's head. It jerks then squawks and bawls, and the baptism is complete. "Sorry," she says, smiling, as she returns. "I love these new beginnings, rebirth, renewal and all of that. I believe it's what makes me important."

Her importance has led to fame and all that comes with it. I ask her how she feels being gawked at and having millions of folks trample across her threshold every year?

"Well, I'm used to it by now. I seem to be a cross between Marilyn Monroe for gawking and Grand Central Station for trampling," she laughs at her self-comparison. "After 142 years, I've been through it all. The thrill of my first years, the nightmare loss of Anton, abandonment, war, and finally a new start." She sighs. "Of course I have visitors who have heart attacks, get sick, faint.

One fellow took a pee in the west corner." She chuckles, and light shines through her stained glass. "Nothing is new to me anymore."

I ask Sagra what her earliest memory is.

She thinks for a moment. "I was inside Anton's head, I remember that." She's referring to the design genius, Antoni Gaudi, whose creation she is. She will often refer to him as just Anton. "I was his vision, like a symphony was inside Beethoven. He wanted me to be a singular design, a church like no one had ever seen before, something unique. Anton wanted to reflect the symmetry he saw in nature. He believed all design was there, already created."

Is that why the columns look like redwood trees and the ceiling supports like branches, I ask? She nods.

"Did you notice my west facade?" She asks. Of course I had. It looks like concrete was splashed in bucketsful against the building and left to run down and congeal. "It's fluttering leaves, you see, like in nature." What of the bowls of fruit atop the parapets?

"Oh my, I think Anton might have gotten a bit into the wine stores when he sketched those! But it's part of my playfulness. Makes me feel a bit like Chiquita Banana with a fruit basket for a hat. He loved the fun of the design, it made him so happy, so I didn't complain. But when he wanted a Christ figure sitting on a giant mushroom I told him a firm no."

She speaks about Anton like a lover. "Oh yes, we were deeply, madly in love. We began our days together, celebrated when my tree columns turned out so beautifully, and commiserated when he tore up a design that didn't work. We lived and breathed as one. He was 73 but with me, he was a young man, full of energy and excitement. Life without him was unthinkable. Until 1926."

She recalls the day her beloved Anton died. He'd just left her in the late afternoon with plans for the east facade racing in his head, she says. "He never paid much attention to the outside world. I was his world and he was mine." He was so distracted he didn't hear the streetcar clanging its warning bell. The car smashed into him, full on. He landed several yards away, unconscious. "He was a bit disheveled and his beard hid much of his face. No one recognized him at first. They took him for a beggar. The clinic they put him in did nothing. When at last someone realized who it was and took him to the real hospital, it was too late. He died." She pauses and glances away, voice shaking. "I died."

The silence lasts several moments. I ask her what happened after she lost him. "I grieved for months, years probably. The loss of him is still sometimes crushing, the memory almost unbearable. I let myself go. Funding stopped and I was abandoned. That time of my life was the darkest."

It was also a dark time for Spain. Three years after Gaudi's death, the financial world collapsed and famine and death came to Spain, followed by another of the Four Horsemen of the Apocalypse: War. The fascist dictator Ferdinand Franco fought and defeated the forces of the Republican government. Hemingway and George Orwell fought with the Republicans, Hitler supported Franco. After millions of deaths, the war ended and Franco became dictator. "Some of his fascist thugs set fire in my office, where Anton had kept my design blueprints. They were destroyed. That was almost as hard to bear as Anton's death," she says in a low voice. "During the war, a few partisans took refuge in me. I hid them in tiny side rooms and in nooks in my towers. It made me feel good, to know at least I was helping people in times of trouble." I ask how long she was abandoned. She brightens.

"Some funds were raised in the 1950s, as I recall, and volunteers cleaned up my inside. The war had been over for 20 years and even though Franco still ruled the country, people began donating to me again. But the money wasn't enough. That depressed me. Then someone in the city government had an idea to copy the Mona Lisa scheme in France!" I look confused and she says she'll explain.

"After World War II, Paris had to lure back her tourists to make money. Someone there arranged for the Mona Lisa to be stolen. It wasn't da Vinci's best work but it was small and easily hidden. Then the authorities flooded the world news media with headlines about the theft. The intense, months-long search dominated cultural news. When the thing was found and returned to the Louvre, the celebrations made headlines again. Tourists worldwide flocked to Paris to see Mona! Still do. It was a sensational success. The marketeers here in Barcelona wanted to do a similar campaign but how do you steal and hide something with hips as big as mine?" She laughs at her own joke. "You can't. So they cloaked me in controversy (I supposedly am hated by the neighbors), tragedy (the loss of my dear Anton), and mystery (did I hide refugees fleeing fascism? yes, but I won't name names). The tourists and the money have been pouring in ever since." She shrugs. "And there it is."

Well, not quite. I ask her how she feels about being nearly completed.

"Oh, that. Small detail. The builders will make sure some construction is always going on. Churches under construction pay no taxes!" She waves her hand. "With my bowls of fruit, exploding stars on top of my tall, skinny towers, my redwood columns and the magical light through my stained glass, I'll always be unique and that brings fame." Is that enough, I ask? Is fame from unique design the most important thing?

She shakes her head a bit. "No. Fame alone is empty. Look," she says as she sweeps her hand across her vast, crowded interior, "my people are Christians, Atheists, Agnostics, Jews, and Muslims. They are all my people. To them I'm Mother Nature in stone, the way Anton made me. Nature means new beginnings, rebirth. That is my true significance, not design, but renewal." She nods to another young couple who have just entered. "Forgive me, I've another baptism." I thank her for her time.

In little side chapels, christenings take place hourly, couples marry, others seek spiritual help, all part of new beginnings, defining the importance of La Sagrada Famila. I watch as the light streams in through the orange, gold, green and blue glass and washes over everyone, rebirth in its wake.

Unrequited Kindness

James Garrison

The summer when I was ten years old, a huge weight fell on my right foot and shattered my big toe, separating the flesh from the bone so that it looked like the meat on a drumstick flopping down from the chicken leg. That event led me first to surgery to restore my big toe and then to a remarkable show of kindness from strangers. I appreciated the surgeon's skill, though he made me sufficiently whole to pass my army physical, but I never understood the reason for kindness from strangers or adequately thanked them—and I'll never forget it.

My brother was seven years my senior and clearly negligent in causing my injury when we tried to move a swimming pool bench with the weight propped against it. Or perhaps I tried to move it alone, but he was there. He was preparing for a swim pageant or something like that, and I was helping him. It was the summer I first took swimming lessons from him in a regular class. The prior year his teaching had consisted of throwing me into water over my head and telling me to swim for it. Then, while I was screaming and going blub, blub, blub, he finally jumped in and pulled me out. Of course, my father was standing there and ordered him to pull me out. Years later my brother told me he regretted doing that. "What?" I asked. "Throwing me in or pulling me out?" I blame my brother for most of the physical injuries and other difficulties of my childhood. (How he became a rocket scientist and head of some NASA center for advanced space propulsion I'll never understand.)

We lived in the house my father built. He began work on it around the time I was born, and it took him two or three years to finish it, before we moved in. It was a cinder block house covered with stucco on the outside and inside. The outside was white, and he "white-washed" it every year or so. The inside was painted whatever colors were available as cheap leftovers at the local hardware store. I recall one year when our kitchen was a shade of purple. Since the cold made the walls sweat in the winter, we had to paint them almost every year. After my father died, my mother paid someone to paint all the walls white, which is how they stayed until she moved fifteen years later to a house nothing like the one my father built.

Anyway, to finish this aside, my father designed and built this house all on his own, dug the cellar, framed it in, set the concrete blocks, installed the plumbing, wired the electricity, everything except the fireplace and chimney for which he had help from a friend. It all worked fairly well, except my mother refused to let us have a fire in the fireplace. Instead, my father built a bookcase in it where we kept a set of cheap, red-bound encyclopedias. I once tried to read them, but I don't remember much beyond "aardvark."

We were living in this house when my brother caused me to crush my toe and go about on crutches for weeks. I never realized that hobbling on crutches with a huge bandage on one's foot could transform me from a ten-year-old, insignificant nuisance, most often told to get lost, into an object of attention and sympathy. Before, I doubt that any adults, other than my parents, or friends of my brother's, ever considered me worthy of attention of any kind. My brother, I'm sure, had considered me an interloper from birth, someone who was best just ignored, unless to tell me he "wouldn't give me air in a bottle" or to call me birdbrain or fart blossom, though I probably returned those in kind. But after my unfortunate injury, his girlfriend gave me a much-coveted Hardy Boys book that cost more than my meager allowance, and a woman I didn't know, and my father and mother certainly didn't know, took me under her wing.

My brother was a genial, good-looking high school senior, and in my recollection, something of a local heart throb, with his nineteen-fifties crewcut and lifeguard tan. He had good grades and lots of friends, and he even got his photograph in the local newspaper from time to time and in the high school yearbook, crowning some teenage girl for something or other. Me jealous? Never.

But I don't think the woman who temporarily adopted the injured waif while his big toe healed had any reason to want to help me because of him. She may have had a connection to the swim pageant or perhaps her daughter went to school with my big brother. She had no children my age, and the daughter was dating some other guy, not my brother. I remember her, my benefactor, making the daughter's date surrender his shoes so that she could shine them. Or maybe she just told him he needed to go shine his shoes himself before he went on a date with her daughter. To me the woman was royalty, or at least a duchess. Or maybe just an angel.

She would pick me up at my house close to the public pool where my brother worked and take me in her car to her house. I remember being enthralled with the beautiful sunroom and the furniture and real shag carpets and the television, but I can't remember how she looked. Just the aura that surrounded her. Perhaps like one of the sitcom housewives in the old fifties television shows, but in color. And she never seemed the passive type. In fact, she always seemed in command. Like telling the teenage boy to shine his shoes, or insisting she shine them for him.

I was surprised my mother would surrender me into the woman's custody, since she was not a relative or even a friend of my mother's. Didn't even go to the same church and may have been Catholic for all I know. My mother was so protective, I never went to a friend's house overnight, or vice versa. In fact, my mother had few friends who came to the house in those days, mostly relatives, of which there were many. I do recall a couple of neighbors who came over to sit on the front lawn with my parents, watching us kids throw sock-covered tennis balls at bats or catch lightning bugs in old mayonnaise jars with holes in their lids. At the time of my injury, my mother was going through severe depression, and had been for the last year, even had electric shock treatments. I wonder if my benefactor/angel knew about that.

No TV, car, telephone—that was how my family lived in 1956—until my mother used her weekly allowance from my father (yep, that's right) to have a telephone installed so that my brother, the high school heartthrob, could talk to his girlfriend. So, I reveled in watching television at the kind woman's house for a few hours and, I'm sure, drinking a Co-cola and eating snacks. And she gave me books: *The Adventures of Robin Hood*, a book of stories about dogs, and maybe a novel by Dickens—I can't remember; but I still have the old, worn Robin Hood book. I can see its faded red cover on my bookshelf.

Then my toe healed completely, though a bit stubby on the end, and my idyll ended. I never saw the woman again, and I cannot remember her name. She never asked for the return of her books—or for thanks. And as an unrefined and self-centered ten-year-old, I never thought to thank her for her kindness.

In my long life, many people have showered me with kindness, and either I've not recognized it or adequately thanked them. In one instance, the benefit provided had consequences that reverberated through my life.

When I was in college, my then girlfriend, a high school senior, ran away from home and rode a bus to Chapel Hill, NC, seeking my help to escape from what she said was an abusive situation. I recalled her father watching television, an old Roy Rogers movie, cleaning his arsenal, the gun parts spread out on the floor and couch beside him, and instantly realized that this could get complicated. I never found out what exactly had happened with the father; my girlfriend made only subtle references to sexual abuse, although a couple were specific, and verbal. Before long, after the girlfriend arrived in Chapel Hill, I heard from home that the father had been storming about in his front yard, waving a .45 and expounding on what he'd do to me. This presented a quandary. Marriage was certainly not in the cards, nor was the girlfriend returning home to whatever the situation there was, at least as far as she, or I, was concerned.

Answering an ad in the local paper, the girlfriend and I visited an old Victorian house, as I remember it, where a room was advertised for rent by a family with two small children. That's how we met Carolista, a friendly and attractive young woman with a poetic name that immediately appealed to me. She started asking questions about the girl's situation, and ended up taking in my girlfriend, without any rent, asking only that she help look after the two young children. The girlfriend confided in Carolista about her abuse at home, and eventually Carolista managed to enroll the girl in high school to complete her senior year—and keep the father at bay. The girlfriend jilted me before graduating from high school, then left Carolista's care to live … I don't know where. I visited Carolista again in the fall that year, and she did not know either. It was the sixties and communes were becoming popular.

Carolista owned a small jewelry store in Chapel Hill and another on the North Carolina Outer Banks, in Nags Head. When my future wife and I were planning our small and inexpensive wedding (in exchange for two tickets to Sao Paulo, objective Rio de Janeiro), we visited Carolista's jewelry store in Chapel Hill to buy wedding rings. She happened to have two gold rings she had crafted before the price of gold went through the roof—it was less than $40 an ounce then. Each of the rings has a lovely design that doesn't quite match the other but complement each other. Sort of like my wife and me. For several reasons, the rings are the most precious things we own.

I searched for Carolista on the web a few years ago and discovered that she had died young, yet she was something of a hero on the Outer Banks of North Carolina. There's even a street named after her and a plaque nearby. She and her children were on the dunes near Nags Head one day in 1973 when she spotted a bulldozer preparing to flatten one of the highest dunes. As she had when she encountered my then-girlfriend and me, she sprang into action. **"North Carolina Woman Who Saved Jockey's Ridge To Be Featured on Highway Historical Marker."** NC Division of Parks and Recreation post on June 26, 2023. The article recounts that:

> On August 15, 1973, [Carolista] Baum courageously positioned herself in the path of a bulldozer sent to remove sand from Jockey's Ridge. Defying the machine's progress and finally engaging in a heartfelt conversation with the bulldozer's operator, the driver departed the dune. …
>
> While local organizations had previously discussed protecting the expansive dune from encroaching development, it was Baum's unwavering determination that transformed the idea into reality. Inspired by her dramatic protest, Baum co-founded the group People to Preserve Jockey's Ridge, rallying support through fundraising initiatives and petition drives to capture the attention of state lawmakers and local officials.

Not long after seeing this article, my wife and I visited the Outer Banks—and there was Carolista's name on a street sign and a marker commemorating her victory. There's a Jockey Ridge State Park now, thanks to Carolista, and she has received well-deserved recognition for her decisive action.

But I never thanked her—or maybe I did and just don't remember it. My wife and I paid for our rings, and we certainly thanked her for those. But as far as the wayward girlfriend? All I can say is that for Carolista's perceptiveness, kindness, and generosity, I am forever thankful. Carolista certainly is *my* hero.

MALLEY

John M. Williams

The pregnancy of Malley's mother, which led to his birth, was unwelcome all around. Neither she, Malley's father, nor what were soon to be Malley's two older brothers had any desire for an additional member of the family, and considered his conception at best a vile accident, at worst a stroke of cosmic vindictiveness.

After his uncelebrated arrival, his father, secretly suspecting this wasn't his doing, simply ignored him; his mother, who wasn't gifted with an inexhaustible supply to begin with, withheld her love; and his brothers tormented him with impunity and righteous indignation.

Some would call that a bad start.

And things didn't get better.

Do the unwanted and despised exude some subliminal chemical that alerts the people waiting in each subsequent phase of life? Apparently so, because the cruelty and ostracism of grade school unfolded inevitably when he got there.

He survived.

In high school the situation grew official with the advent of the "Hate Malley" society—not exactly a club, more of an underground conspiracy enabling everyone besides Malley to have a Malley: someone to whom all recognition, support, love, affection, and friendship was denied. People need that.

But at least they recognized a "him." Which for a shaky moment enabled him to experience the first spasms of ego formation.

Then high school ended and that changed. The world ceased to hate, but just forgot him, which killed the ego thing and gave him some breathing room.

He found a job managing a warehouse for a small manufacturing company. A solo job at which he became so proficient no one else was needed. He had no way, and no need, to tell time—he just appeared at work and left punctually, went to bed, woke up, ate, likewise.

Malley found a rental house within walking distance of his job, ate very little, and had almost no needs or wants. He had no car, no computer, no phone, no television, and though once or twice he had heard a strain of music that kind of roused him, he had never really caught on to the music thing either.

So he was able to save the better part of his salary. As the years went by, his weekly walks to make a deposit at the bank resulted in a substantial sum, and when the old man renting him the house had a stroke, his family offered to sell Malley the house, so he bought it.

As he grew into middle age, luckily the manufacturing company survived the moody economy and stayed in business, and he kept his job. He didn't want, and never bothered to imagine, any other.

Except for the occasional mildly curious glance of a random stranger, or someone in the grocery store or bank who had been seeing him there for years and paused to wonder, it was as though he had dissolved so deeply into the fabric of existence that no one was any longer aware of him.

He was the only free man in town.

Since it was so empty, Malley's life was full. At the bifurcations of daily life—turning to the left or right, entering the first or second door, stepping or not on a crunchy leaf, for example—his mind habitually dramatized a flash projection of every path not taken: the different perception of reality from another angle, an alternate sequence of events, an uncrunched leaf being blown by the wind under a camellia bush where it could peacefully remember its chlorophyll-fattened days in the sun. His mind was a theater, constantly playing scenarios that either might have, could have, should have, maybe somewhere else had, or never would have, happened. Whenever he closed his eyes, places he had never been, people he had never seen, situations he could never have purposely imagined, materialized effortlessly, ceaselessly, and he just watched.

Time was equally footloose in his timeless mind. He often found himself in the far future experiencing the present like a memory, walking through a world dreamy because it had already happened. At other times he experienced the present from the past, simultaneously seeing his projection of what the future might be, as it didn't match but, as it were, shadowed what the future had settled for.

Some days he saw something when he looked in the mirror, some days he didn't. When he did, he experienced what he would have called humor if he'd had need of a word for it, which he didn't. He would probably have said that sensation was the essence of everything, if he'd had the inclination to formulate a philosophy, which he didn't.

Walking onto the endlessly interesting blank canvas of his leaf and twig and acorn littered driveway after work, no eyes watching him, alive in no one's mind, he might see a squirrel high in the water oak and inevitably find himself seeing the world from that perspective, sharing the squirrel's consciousness. Same with birds. He never tired of seeing the stationary world through their darting eyes. Or the ants at his feet, into whose intricate kingdoms his imagination burrowed. Or he might notice a twig in the yard and experience its time-lapse decay back into the earth—or its disintegration by lawn mower blades, the pieces searching for other parts of itself, haunted by the ghosts of those days of being a twig. He would share the life experience of the beans he ate for dinner, from the sprouting out of the warm moist earth, to the hands picking them, to their entering his digestive system and becoming a part of him.

After dinner, weather permitting, he would sit on the back porch and watch the sun set, just as he would watch it rise out his front window in the mornings. He never got tired of that slow, suspenseful drama. He could see, as from a distance, the great ponderous globe slowly creaking around, could see the speck of himself as it turned into or out of the light. He spent endless hours trying to reconcile the vertical depiction of the world with its horizontal perception. Weather not permitting, he might spend the time in the clouds.

What did Malley believe in?

A meaningless question. And a waste of time.

He didn't believe in anything, which is how he could believe in everything.

Dirty Work

Mike Nemeth

At the crack of the bat, I turned and ran for the outfield fence. Over my left shoulder, I watched the ball climb over the sun and hesitate at its apex before hurtling toward the warning track far ahead of me.

I pumped my arms and dug my spikes into the soft field but I wouldn't reach the fence in time. After three long strides, I pivoted to face home plate and located the ball falling from the sky like a meteor crashing through earth's atmosphere. Fear froze the blood in my veins. I stretched my glove hand toward the heavens and jumped as high as my legs could propel me, but I caught only a handful of spring air. Ten feet behind me the ball collided with the outfield wall, bounced once on the warning track, and caromed off my shin.

Ignoring the sting of the ball, I scuttled on hands and knees to retrieve the ball, watched the batter round third base and head for home. I rose and fired the ball in one fluid motion. The ball sailed over the cutoff man, ricocheted off the pitcher's mound, and bounded toward the catcher. He left his position and smothered the ball on the infield grass as the batter slid across the plate behind him.

Game over.

I rested on my haunches, holding my breath to stave off tears of shame. After several minutes of self-pity, I chanced a glance around the field and spotted Dad standing on the third base line. I hadn't expected him to show up. Now I wished he hadn't.

I joined my teammates, their faces long and sad, in a line, congratulating the ebullient winners like we'd been taught by our coach. When Allen, our pitcher, passed the kid who hit the home run, he spat, "It was just a stupid fly ball."

A stupid fly ball I didn't catch. *My teammates blame me for losing the game.* It's the first game of the season, on the first Saturday of summer, and I was already a failure.

The batter shoved Allen and a scuffle ensued, but coaches quickly separated the two teams and the players dispersed. I shuffled toward Dad and my coach who waited for me with their arms folded across their chests.

When I was within earshot, Dad said, "You run too long in one place."

I wondered if that was a professional opinion. After all, he was an engineer.

"He shouldn't have looked back," the coach said. "It slowed him down. We teach 'em to run to the spot, then pick up the ball 'cause you run faster looking straight ahead."

Dad nodded in full agreement. "He didn't get a good jump on the ball."

I stopped in front of Dad. "I read the ball off the bat. It was way over my head."

I turned to my coach. "You had me playing too shallow."

Dad smacked the back of my head hard enough to knock off my cap.

"You'll play where the coach tells you to play, young man."

"Frank, not all boys are cut out for center field." The coach picked my cap out of the dirt, dusted it off, and set it on my head. "Eddie doesn't have the speed to cover center field no matter where I position him."

I shuffled my feet, not sure if I should interlope again or catch up to my teammates. Fear of their ridicule paralyzed me. I wanted to play organized baseball because it was Dad's favorite sport. The mistake I made was wanting to be a center fielder because Mickey Mantle was Dad's favorite player. The mistake the coach made was giving me a try.

"Wouldn't surprise me if you cut him," Dad said to the coach. "Struck out twice today."

The coach shrugged. "He got a walk, scored a run."

"He didn't hit a lick in Little League so don't expect him to hit for you, either. His brother, Danny, is the baseball player in our family."

"Sure. I remember Danny from his Youth League days. That boy was a homer just waiting to happen."

"He was a star in high school ball. He's sure to get a scholarship to play in college."

"Well, Eddie here has one skill that will keep him on my team." The coach gripped my shoulder in a fatherly way. "Did you see that throw? All the way from the warning track? Your kid's got a cannon for an arm."

Dad scoffed. "You're not going to try to make him a pitcher, are you?"

The coach spat out his chewing tobacco. "Nah, but I need a catcher." He cupped a hand to his mouth and leaned toward Dad as though whispering a secret. "Our catcher should have waited for the throw and blocked the plate." He straightened. "And I'd like to have a catcher with a gun." The coach gave me an appraising look. "If he ain't afraid of the ball that is."

Catcher! The position is reserved for kids who can't run and can't hit but are willing to demean themselves by chasing wild pitches around the backstop. But it's either play catcher or get cut from the team.

"I'm not afraid of the ball, sir." I puffed out my chest in a show of mock confidence.

"That's what I want to hear." The coach flashed a mouthful of brown tobacco-stained teeth and gave my shoulder an encouraging smack.

"Then I guess you're a damn catcher." Dad shook his head and walked away.

The coach shrugged. "We'll give it a try. Let's get your equipment."

I followed him to the dugout where he filled a canvas bat bag with shin guards, chest protector, face mask, and a padded catcher's mitt. The equipment was old, the seams frayed and torn, the straps stretched and no longer elastic, the edges worn smooth. But they were my ticket to play Youth League baseball. I walked home alone with the "tools of ignorance" slung over my shoulder.

As I lugged the equipment to my room, Danny stuck his head out his bedroom door. "You must be the chubbiest kid on the team. They always make the chubby kid play catcher."

***

Dad didn't waste his time watching a damn catcher play Youth League baseball. On game days I snuck away before he could make excuses for not coming to the game.

According to Dad, the Brooklyn Dodgers had scouted him as a high school player in rural Iowa, but when Hitler invaded Poland and war was imminent, he had abandoned my grandfather's pig farm and enlisted in the Navy. It was Danny's burden to make up for Dad's sacrifice. My baseball games would never be enough.

Dad was right about my hitting, of course. However, I learned to look fierce in the batter's box and milk wild pitchers for walks. I can't count the times the coach said, "A walk is as good as a hit." I knew—all players knew—a walk was only as good as a hit for a player who couldn't hit. I hadn't gotten a hit all season and my teammates had begun to grumble. Since no one else wanted to play catcher, the coach told the grumblers to shut their yaps.

The fact that I hadn't gotten a hit was on my mind as I came to bat with two outs in the bottom of the last inning, losing by a run, with Timmy on third base. The coach couldn't pinch hit for me because if we tied the game, we'd have no one else able, or willing, to play catcher. He counted on my ability to draw a walk and keep the game alive. With the pitch count full—three balls and two strikes—the odds were good that I could draw another walk, giving the next batter in our lineup a chance to drive in the tying run. But this pitcher had alternated balls and strikes so the next pitch was just as likely to be a strike. I couldn't live with the embarrassment of a called third strike to end the game. I *had* to swing at the pitch.

And I did. For a microsecond the bat and ball shared the same space and the ball rebounded off the bat. It flew in a graceful arc, over the outstretched arm of the pitcher, between opposing infielders, beyond second base, and onto the outfield grass. The tying run came home from third base and my coach slapped me on my butt as I reached first base. Our next batter, Allen, slugged a home run and won the game for us.

When I crossed home plate my teammates were there, waiting for Allen. I got caught up in the crowd of players congratulating our hero, and the melee gravitated toward the chain link fence behind home plate where I was crushed against it by the jubilant celebration. The sharp point of a twisted metal thread ripped my uniform and gashed my upper arm. It dripped a stream of bright red blood.

I bounced into the house with a wide grin and a bloody arm.

"Oh, my God," Mom screamed. "Let me fix it."

As she applied Mercurochrome and murmured soothing encouragement, Dad said, "Stop babying him."

Mom ignored him and covered the cut with an unnecessarily large piece of gauze and wrapped an athletic bandage around my arm far too many times.

"I drove in the tying run and scored the winning run." Technically, this was true, but I didn't reveal that the next batter hit a walk-off home run and was the object of the celebration.

"Looks more like you've been in a fight," Dad said.

"No, during the celebration I got crushed against the backstop. I thought you'd be proud of me."

"So, the blind squirrel found an acorn. Will we have to pay for the uniform?"

For the first time in my life, I called him a dirty name. Not out loud, of course. We didn't have to pay for the ripped baseball uniform. Mom stitched up the L-shaped tear, and I wore my lucky uniform to every game.

***

In the last game of the season, we played for the championship against the team that had beaten us in the opening game of the season—the loss attributed to my slow feet.

Leading by two runs in the bottom of the last inning, with two outs and a runner on second base, our coach gathered us on the mound for final instructions. Their next batter would be the kid who hit the ball over my head to win the first game of the season.

"Let's end this right here. Give him somethin' to hit, make him put the ball in play," the coach told Allen. To the rest of us, he said, "You do your jobs and we'll be champions."

As I trotted back to my place behind home plate, the batter took vicious practice swings in the on-deck circle while sneering at me. "Gonna be just like last time," he warned.

"Nah, this time I'm behind the plate, not in the outfield."

"You couldn't catch your momma if she was wearing combat boots. That's why you're a catcher."

I didn't let him get into my head. I squatted behind him and signaled Allen we were ready for play. Allen did as he was told and laid a fat pitch down the middle of the plate.

The batter swung so hard his helmet flew off and he dropped to one knee in the batter's box. The ball was struck hard, but the batter had overswung and topped it. Like a laser beam it streaked along the ground as the batter got to his feet and stumbled toward first base.

Our shortstop nearly made the play. The ball kicked off the heel of his glove and ricocheted toward the left field foul line. The runner from second base scored easily, reducing our margin to a single run. Our fielders chased the fleeing ball like cops chasing a purse snatcher. Timmy, our left fielder, finally smothered the ball in foul territory as the batter rounded third base. I tossed my mask aside and planted a foot on either side of the plate. Timmy's throw was strong and true but a few feet short of the plate, nearly striking the runner as he began his slide.

Ignoring the sliding runner, I concentrated on the ball, caught it with two hands and dropped to my knees. The batter crashed into me, spikes first and the impact flipped me onto my back. The crowd groaned and gasped. Time stood still as we waited for the umpire's call. When the dust cleared, the umpire reached down and turned my glove over to reveal the ball resting on my chest protector.

He punched the sky and bellowed, "He's out!"

The crowd went wild. Lying there for a glorious second, I absorbed the cheers from the stands. My dream had come true: we were champions.

The once-cocky batter skittered away. He knew what was about to happen and so did I. Before I could stand, I was mobbed by fourteen delirious teammates, crushed at the bottom of a delicious dogpile, covered in red dirt and borrowed sweat.

When my teammates pulled me to my feet, I discovered that my uniform had been ripped again, and my thigh had been sliced by the batter's spikes.

I limped to the dugout to remove my equipment for the last time and heard a gasp from behind me.

"Let's get you to the emergency room, young man," the coach said. "You'll need stitches."

"No way, Coach. I'm leaving it just like this for everyone to see."

He shook his head in the way fathers do when they disapprove of what their son is doing but are proud of it too. "I'll walk you home and explain to your dad," he said.

When Mom saw the blood on my leg, she shrieked, "Oh, my God!" She took a step to hug me and thought better of it. She placed her hands on either side of my face, careful not to get dirt and blood on her sundress and gave me an air kiss. "I'll fix you up."

As Mom headed to the bathroom for some medical supplies, Dad shuffled up to me. "What happened?"

"I blocked the plate and got spiked."

"He won the game for us and the championship to boot," the coach said. "I feel pretty smart now. He was the best dang catcher in the league. He wasn't afraid of the bat, foul tips, or sliding runners. No wild pitches got past him and no runner ever stole a base. Made the All-Star team."

Dad made a sound that betrayed a combination of disbelief and confusion. "You're joking, right? Has he learned to hit?"

"There's more to the game than hitting, sir," the coach said. "Every team needs someone to do the dirty work."

Star Crossed Lovers

Robin Prince Monroe

Adorned with scrim of clouds and mist,
her face reflected in shining sand,
Sun dresses in violet, rose, and gold preparing for her beloved.

Moon rises clothed in dusky gray,
delighted to see her waiting there,
His silver fingers stretch over the water, sprinkling gifts of sparkling stars.

He reaches to touch Sun's gleaming face.
Her golden arms fling open wide.

Then bound by time, Sun pulls away,
And sadly, softly nods good-bye.

The sea oats whisper to the wind.
Bright tears splash waves with toppling light
Smaller now but hopeful still,
Moon bravely lights another night.

If I Could Go Back

J. B. Hogan

If I could go back to when
you were here, before you left,
before the quiet, the aching quiet,
when we still talked, when we
still laughed and you were there,
we had snapshots of the moon,
the sky, the neighbor's bright lights
that bothered you and the cat,
and brought light to the night,
night that shone on my dark soul
that you had so easily captured but
was too dark, too changeable to
override all the reasons
that you left, left me here
in the future, where all I can do
is look back, look back to the time
when you were here, before you left,
before the emptiness, the aching emptiness,
where we no longer talk, no longer laugh,
no longer matter – save in my dark,
unfulfilled and unhappy dreams.

About the Authors

Deborah-Zenha Adams is an award-winning author of novels, short fiction, CNF, and poetry. She served as executive editor of *Oconee Spirit Press* for ten years, and is currently a reader for *Boomerli*t. Her writing has appeared or is forthcoming in *Roanoke Review, Litmosphere*: a journal of Charlotte Lit, *WELL READ Magazine, Susurrus,* and other journals. You're invited to visit her website. www.Deborah-Adams.com.

Rickie Zayne Ashby is retired and lives near Bowling Green, Kentucky. He is the author of three books, including *Walton's Creek, Land of Our Fathers Volumes I and II.*

Hubert Blair Bonds, a native of Kannapolis, NC, has lived in Atlanta, GA for more than 30 years. He is retired from the federal government with 34 years of service. Currently serving as Curator at the East Point Historical Society, his hobbies include gardening, film history, and writing.

Rita Welty Bourke is the author of *Kylie's Ark: The Making of a Veterinarian* and *Islomanes of Cumberland Island.* Crossings is forthcoming in the spring of 2026. She's married to songwriter Rory Bourke and is the mother of three daughters. Visit her website at RitaWeltyBourke.com.

Born and raised in New York City's grittiness, Brittingham spent a large segment of her adult years in the blue skies and humidity of South Florida. Today, she resides along the magnificent (and sometimes tumultuous) shores of Lake Michigan, which offer ample opportunities for creative contemplation. She has published essays in the *Hartford Courant; short stories* in Florida Literary Foundation's hardcover anthology, *Paradise*; in the 1996 Florida First Coast Writers' Festival, and in Britain's World Wide Writers. In Anthology of Short Stories-Autumn 2021 was *Loose End*s. Her essays *Feed the Beast* and *Judas Season* and *The Arts and Bad Words* have been published in *WELL READ Magazine*. The short story *Something of Significance* was printed in the Culture Cult Anthology, *Creatures of Habit* in April 2024.

John Drudge is a social worker working in the field of disability management and holds degrees in social work, rehabilitation services, and psychology. He is the author of seven books of poetry: *March* (2019), *The Seasons of Us* (2019), *New Days* (2020), *Fragments* (2021), *A Long Walk* (2023), *A Curious Art* (2024) and *Sojourns* (2024) .His work has appeared widely in literary journals, magazines, and anthologies internationally. John is also a Pushcart Prize and Best of the Net nominee and lives in Caledon Ontario, Canada with his wife and two children.

Don Edwards has previously published five books of poetry. Mr Edwards is also the founding member of True Gospel Bookstore which records his poems as songs which are available to hear on Spotify and all streaming services. Mr Edwards lives in Los Angeles.

James Garrison practiced law before writing three award-winning novels: *QL 4*, set in the Mekong Delta in 1970, *The Safecracker*, a legal thriller, and *What Seems True*, inspired by an unresolved 1979 murder in Texas. His latest work, *Ruminations: stories, essays, and poems*, was released in 2024. His prose and poems have appeared in literary magazines and anthologies. www.jamesgarrison-author.com.

Malcolm Glass has published fifteen books of poetry and non-fiction. His work has appeared in many journals, including *Poetry, The Sewanee Review*, and *The Write Launch*. In 2018, Finishing

Line Press published his chapbook *Mirrors, Myths, and Dreams*; and next year Finishing Line will release his triple-hybrid collection, *Her Infinite Variety*. Also an artist and photographer, Glass has had artwork juried into dozens of exhibitions and galleries, including The Hilliard Gallery, Art Fluent, Photo Artfolio, and Nuu Contemporary Art. His work has won dozens of awards, from honorable mention to Best of Show.

Aaron Goodman is a writer based in White Rock, British Columbia. His first novel, *The Imbroglio of Aziel Glogowski,* has yet to be published, and he is completing a second book.

Julie Green is a retired museum curator, wife, mom, lifelong choral singer, and radical arts advocate. She writes in her living room with her dog Tashi who rarely provides inspiration and sleeps a lot. She is currently finishing a novel and putting together a chapbook. Her work has appeared in several journals including *Slant, The Reach of Song, Circle of Women* (Emory University), and *Naugatuck River Review*. She is the 2023 and 2024 recipient of the Herbert Shippey Award for Excellence in Southern Poetry, and the Low Country Award for Short Story given by the Southeastern Writers Association.

Alaina Hammond is a poet, playwright, fiction writer, and visual artist. Her poems, short stories, and paintings have been published both online and in print. Publications include *Littoral Magazine, Third Wednesday Magazine, [Alternate Route], Paddler Press, Verse-Virtual, Macrame Literary Journal, Sublunary Review, Quail Bell Magazine, Assignment Literary Magazine, Superpresent, Jelly Squid, redrosethorns*, and *Flash Frog*. @alainaheidelberger on Instagram.

In September of 2011 Gallery, an imprint of Simon & Schuster, published Ann Hite's first novel, *Ghost on Black Mountain*. In 2012 this novel was shortlisted for the Townsend Prize, Georgia's oldest literary award. In the same year, *Ghost on Black Mountain* won Hite Georgia Author of the Year. She went on to publish four more novels, a novella, memoir, and most recently *Haints On Black Mountain: A Haunted Short Story Collection* from Mercer University Press. In December 2022, *Haints On Black Mountain* was one of ten finalist for the Townsend Prize. The collection was a Bronze Winner in Foreword Indie Award 2023 and Georgia Author of the Year Second Place Winner for Short Stories 2023. Ann received a scholarship to the Appalachian Writers Workshop Hindman Settlement in the summer of 2020 and was invited back in 2021. Her passion for history influences all her work.

J. B. Hogan has been published in a number of journals including the *Blue Lake Review, Crack the Spine, Copperfield Review, Lothlorien Poetry Journal, Well Read Magazine*, and *Aphelion*. His eleven books include *Bar Harbor, Mexican Skies, Living Behind Time, Losing Cotton*, and *The Apostate*. He lives in Fayetteville, Arkansas.

Mary Kendall is first a reader of books across the genres and, second, a writer of fiction. She brings her background in history-related fields to her writing along with some Celtic story-telling genes. Her published novels include *The Spinster's Fortune, Campbell's Boy, Bottled Secrets of Rosewood* and, an upcoming release, *The Accidental Heiress*.

Zoé Mahfouz is a multi-talented artist—an award-winning bilingual actress, screenwriter, and writer whose works span fiction, nonfiction, and poetry, featured in 40+ literary magazines worldwide. Her comedic scripts, including *I Follow You* and *Commercial Actress*, have garnered recognition at festivals like Hollywood Comedy Shorts, Filmmatic, Scriptation Showcase, and Toronto International Nollywood Film Festival.

Dawn Major's book, *The Bystanders*, was a finalist for 2024 Georgia Author of the Year for Best First Novel. Major is an associate editor at *Southern Literary Review* and a co-editor at *WELL READ Magazine* and serves on the board at Broadleaf Writers Association. In addition, Major is a member of the Horror Writers

Association and a member of M'ville, an Atlanta-based artist salon. Major is also part of Team Gay, a group dedicated to preserving the legacy of the late author William Gay. She lives in Atlanta, GA with her family and is currently working on a horror novel called *Chronicles in Dandy Land.*

Celia Miles, retired NC community college instructor, lives and writes in Asheville. Her Appalachian heritage, her interest in old water-powered grist mills, and her exploration of Britain's neolithic stone circles are evident in her thirteen novels, two collections of short stories, and some poetry. and photography. website: celiamiles.com.

Robin Prince Monroe delights in writing for children; and has authored seven picture books, a middle grade novel, and a chapter book. Recently released titles for grownups include, *Ridiculously Easy Crockpot Recipes, Ridiculously Easy Creative Problem Solving, Time Trees and Grandpa's Knees*, and *Loss of a Loved One.* Her work has also appeared in *Guideposts*, and *Money Matters*. Www.RobinPrinceMonroe.com.

Mike Nemeth, a Vietnam veteran and former high-tech executive, writes love stories tucked inside murder mysteries. *The Undiscovered Country, Parker's Choice*, and *A Tissue of Lies* are multiple award winners. Mike's works have appeared in *The New York Times, Georgia Magazine, Augusta Magazine, Southern Writers' Magazine*, and *Deep South Magazine. Creative Loafing* named him Atlanta's Best Local Author for 2018.

Gregg Norman lives and writes in a lakeside cottage in Manitoba, Canada, with his wife and a small dog who runs the joint. His poetry has been placed in journals and literary magazines in Canada, USA, UK, Australia and India. He is also the author of four published novels and a novella.

JoyAnne O'Donnell is an author of five poetry books available on Amazon including *Winds of Time, Spring & Summers Veil, Palace of Enchanted Day and Night, Heavens Medal*, and *Summer In The Breeze.* JoyAnne has twice been nominated for The Pushcart Prize.

DeLane Phillips is a southern writer, former teacher, empty nester, and dog mom of Mac the Dachshund and Lovey the Terrier. Much of her writing is inspired by rural life from her childhood on a farm in Monroe, Georgia and the various characters of the small southern towns she has traveled through and lived in. She continues to reside in Georgia.

Steve Putnam's short fiction has appeared in *Main Street Rag, Whiskey Island, Magazine*, and Scribes Valley Publishing anthologies. His novel, *Academy of Reality*, a 2019 Faulkner-Wisdom Competition finalist in New Orleans, was recently released by Madville Publishing.

Francine Rodriguez has three previously published novels, and her last novel, *A Woman's Story* was the silver medal winner in the International Latino Book Awards for 2022. She also has several short stories published in anthologies such as *Taboos and Transgressions, Works in Progress, WELL READ's Best of 2023*, and in various literary journals. Her short story entitled; *An Hour in The Life of a Five-year-Old Pool Player* was nominated for a Pushcart Award in 2024, and she's currently preparing a script for Call Sheet Productions on several stories in *A Woman's Story*.

Mike Ross has flipped burgers at Burger Chef, been a County Jail administrator, a German teacher for 35 years, and a tour guide for 45 years. He lives in Michigan, with his wife, Dianna (an awesome editor), and has loads of kids and grandkids. He is a traveler, runner and skier but his first love is writing.

Jake Sheff is a pediatrician and US Air Force veteran. He's published a full-length collection of formal poetry, *A Kiss to Betray the Universe* (White Violet Press), along with three chapbooks: *Looting Versailles* (Alabaster Leaves Publishing), *The Rites of*

Tires (SurVision) and *The Seagull's First One Hundred Seguidillas* (Alien Buddha Press).

Jennifer Susan Smith, a retired speech-language pathologist, resides in northwest Georgia. Jennifer's writing is published in *The Mildred Haun Review, The Bluebird Word, WELL READ Magazine*, and *San Antonio Review*, among others. She is chairman of Alpha Delta Kappa Pages and Pearls Book Club, and holds membership in Chattanooga Writers' Guild.

Rachid Toumi (hemingwayagadir@gmail.com / rachid.toumi@edu.uiz.ac.ma) got his doctorate in 2023 from the Faculty of Letters and Human Sciences, Ibn Zohr University, Morocco ("The Laboratory of Values, Society and Development"). His doctoral thesis is on the theme of Identity and expatriation in the works of the American authors, Ernest Hemingway and James Baldwin. He completed an MA program in English titled "Race, Ethnicity, and Alterity in Literature and Culture" in 2007 at the same faculty. Rachid is a former high school teacher of English at the Ministry of Education in Morocco. He currently holds the position of Assistant Professor at Ibn Zohr University, Morocco. He has published articles on modern American fiction (https://orcid.org/0009-0007-2045-8480).

Mike Turner is a poet living on the U.S. Gulf Coast. He has over 350 poems published in over 75 journals and anthologies including *Well Read Magazine*; his lyric, *Sense of Peace*, was awarded the Alabama Writers' Cooperative's 2023 Roger Williams Peace Prize. Mike's book, *Visions and Memories*, is available on Amazon.

Micah Ward writes, runs, and enjoys craft beer in middle Tennessee. His short stories have been published in *Well Read* and in anthologies produced by the Colorado Springs Fiction Writers and the Amelia Island Writers clubs. Micah has received three Honorable Mentions from the Lorian Hemingway Short Story Competition and has been nominated for a Pushcart Prize. He was also named Outstanding Club Writer of the year by the Road Runners Club of America for his articles on running.

John M. Williams is a mentor in the Reinhardt University MFA Creative Writing program. He was named Georgia Author of the Year for First Novel in 2002 for Lake Moon (Mercer UP). He has written and co-written numerous plays, with several local productions, and published a variety of stories, essays, and reviews through the years. His and co-author Rheta Grimsley Johnson's play *Hiram: Becoming Hank*, about the formative years of singer Hank Williams, has enjoyed several productions. His most recent books are *Village People: Sketches of Auburn* (Solomon and George 2016), and *Atlanta Pop in the 50s, 60s, and 70s: The Magic of Bill Lowery* (with Andy Lee White) (The History Press 2019), *Monroeville and the Stage Production of "To Kill a Mockingbird"* (The History Press 2023), and his just-released novel *End Times* (Sartoris Literary Group 2023). Other publications can be found on his website at johnmwilliams.net, which hosts his blog, johnmwilliams.net/blog. He lives in LaGrange, Georgia.

Neth Williams is an award-winning paralegal who has used legal research and writing experience to pen hundreds of articles for business firms, marketing companies, and healthcare providers. His poetry has been published in *Stray Words Magazine* (UK) and *Black Coffee Poetry* (Australia). His storytelling was shared across Nashville, TN, where he performed on many stages, including Zanies Comedy Club.

Souad Zakarani - Poetess & translator. Publications in Anthologie : *Frühlings Anthologie 2025* beim Thomas Opfermann, Lyrischer Lorbeer'24 ,"Regenbogeninsel" Anthologie, *Im Fadenkreuz der Archetypen, Märchen, Sex & Gender* beim Wiener Verlag.. 4-times successful publication of Contemporary Poetry beim Brentano Gesellschaft, Frankfurter Bibliothek. Essays & Poems in Magazines: *KKL Magazine /Bạrcelona Adabia/ Raven Cage / Poetry Planet / Global Poets and Poetry.*

Leslie Zemeckis is a best-selling author, actress, and award-winning documentarian and TEDx speaker. Critically acclaimed films include *Behind the Burly Q*, the award-winning *Bound by Flesh, Mabel, Mabel, Tiger Trainer* and *Grandes Horizontales*. Books include *Behind the Burly Q*, (an Amazon Editor's Pick), *Goddess of Love Incarnate; the Life of Stripteuse Lili St. Cyr* and *Feuding Fan Dancers* (a SCIBA finalist for best bio of the year). She was honored with the Ellis Island Medal of Honor for "sharing and preserving stories of women who were once marginalized and stigmatized.

About the artist

Malcolm Glass has published fifteen books of poetry and non-fiction. His work has appeared in many journals, including "Poetry," "The Sewanee Review," and "The Write Launch." In 2018, Finishing Line Press published his chapbook Mirrors, Myths, and Dreams; and next year Finishing Line will release his triple-hybrid collection, *Her Infinite Variety*.

Also an artist and photographer, Glass has had artwork juried into dozens of exhibitions and galleries, including The Hilliard Gallery, Art Fluent, Photo Artfolio, and Nuu Contemporary Art. His work has won dozens of awards, from honorable mention to Best of Show.

WELL READ is looking for submissions from writers and artists who have stories to tell. We combine new and established voices from diverse backgrounds and celebrate different perspectives. We want people who aren't afraid to shake things up, speak their mind, and share their humanity.

No prompts or themes - no boundaries

www.wellreadmagazine.com

www.ingramcontent.com/pod-product-compliance
Lightning Source LLC
LaVergne TN
LVHW090602110826
845146LV00001B/227